The Urbana Free Library

To renew materials call
217-367-4057

7=03

AN INTRIGUING MURDER

AN INTRIGUING MURDER

Roderic Jeffries

This first world edition published in Great Britain 2002 by
SEVERN HOUSE PUBLISHERS LTD of
9–15 High Street, Sutton, Surrey SM1 1DF.
This first world edition published in the USA 2003 by
SEVERN HOUSE PUBLISHERS INC of
595 Madison Avenue, New York, N.Y. 10022.

British Library Cataloguing in Publication Data

Jeffries, Roderic, 1926-
    An intriguing murder. - (An Inspector Alvarez novel)
    1.   Alvarez, Enrique, Inspector (Fictitious character) - Fiction
    2.   Police - Spain - Fiction
    3.   Majorca (Spain) - Fiction
    4.   Detective and mystery stories
    I.   Title
    813.5'4 [F]

    ISBN 0-7278-5907-2

Typeset by Palimpsest Book Production Ltd.,
Polmont, Stirlingshire, Scotland.
Printed and bound in Great Britain by
MPG Books Ltd., Bodmin, Cornwall.

Contents

One

The sky was cloudless and even in the shade of the covered patio, the temperature was in the middle nineties. To the west, a contrail marked another planeload of tourists approaching the airport and their daydreams.

Laura broke a silence which had lasted for a couple of minutes. 'We mustn't forget Wednesday.'

'Or we'll miss it?' Locke asked. They had each learned a way of dulling memories and his was facetiousness. He picked up his glass and drained it. 'Can I get you another?'

'Only a small one. If I don't get lunch soon, it'll be tea time.'

'Then we'll have tea at supper time.'

'How Winifred would be aghast at so casual an attitude.'

'After a couple of months living here, she'd be as relaxed as the rest of us.'

'And I'd be a nervous wreck.'

He watched a humming-bird hawk-moth working the small flowers of the lantana which formed a low hedge beyond the lawn which backed the swimming pool. Did insects have memories? . . . He stood, picked up the glasses, crossed the patio and entered the large sitting room, which was separated from the dining room by an open archway. On the bookcase by the television was the

1

remote control for the air-conditioning unit on the outside wall and he used this to set the temperature at 21 and start the machine, ensuring their meal would be eaten in comfort. That done, he continued on through to the kitchen and descended into the cellar. Few houses were built with cellars and the fact that Ca Na Aila had one epitomized for him the Mallorquins' resourcefulness and explained how they had survived the many invasions over the centuries. The house plans had specified the dimensions of the cisterna, which would collect the rain water off the many roofs, to be built under the kitchen, but as was customary, the man in charge of the earth digger had not bothered to consult them; by the time he had finished excavating, the hole was far larger than required. When this had been pointed out to the builder, he had replied that as the English were known to enjoy wine, he had decided to add a cellar alongside the cisterna and, as a mark of friendship, would increase the agreed estimate by only a very little . . .

Locke poured out two gins, added tonic, returned to the kitchen, brought a tray of ice out of the large refrigerator, and dropped three cubes into each glass. Back on the patio, he handed Laura her glass, sat. 'You haven't explained why we have to remember Wednesday.'

'We're invited to Scott's party. I did tell you that.'

'Only once and as you're always reminding me, I have to be told something three times before it sinks in. Are you finding him any more acceptable?'

She frowned, as she often did when thinking what to say, and he realized how the facial lines were beginning to betray her age. He usually saw her as little older than when they'd married. Not classically beautiful, but notably attractive with blue eyes, a retroussé nose, a mouth which hinted at a passionate temperament, and the warmth of her nature evident. Those were the days when the future could be golden because it was unknown . . .

She said slowly: 'I suppose I'm never completely at ease with him because I have the impression that behind the mask of easy, amusing friendliness, there's a very different man; probably, he's cut a few throats in his time, metaphorically speaking, but that won't make him unique. Most of the other wealthy expats would almost certainly prefer at least some of their past to remain hidden.'

'Give him his due, he throws a generous party.'

'Which fact is far more important than his character?'

'Certainly more relevant to his guests.'

'Have you ever wondered why he serves champagne rather than cava, as everyone else does?'

'I never question pleasure.'

'I think it's because he's showing us all he can afford what others can't and that makes him feel superior.'

'That's really damning the man!'

'His buffet meals are right over the top.'

'Are they?'

'You don't remember the last time we were there? The only luxury not on offer was caviare. Either he doesn't like it or he reckons none of us has had the chance to learn to. Adela remarked she felt like the beggar at the rich man's feast.'

'I imagine she said that as she had a second helping of lobster.'

She picked up her glass. 'Women can be such fools!' She drank.

'A careful no comment unless your remark referred to Adela.'

'Do you remember the blonde who seemed to think she was Scarlett O'Hara?'

'Wasn't Scarlett raven-haired?. . . No, I can't recall her.'

3

'You couldn't keep your eyes off her.'

'Then was she the one who wore a dress which looked as if it might be transparent?'

'And you spent a long time trying to discover if this was an optical illusion . . . Diana told me she was so certain Scott was going to marry her, she was telling people how she'd redecorate his house.'

'That must have alarmed him so much, he dropped her for the next one before he'd planned.'

'He sees women merely as vessels for his satisfaction.'

'Rich men have always enjoyed yachting.'

'If you became rich, would you treat women with contempt?'

'Would I be given the chance?'

'By me? Not bloody likely.' She finished her drink. 'I'll go and get the meal. It's only cold meat and salad.'

'Who wants anything more in this heat?'

'No doubt you'll provide an answer at the party,' she observed dryly. She stood. 'Are we going to eat here or inside?'

'I've switched on the air-conditioning.'

'Then will you lay the table?'

She went indoors, but he did not immediately follow her. He viewed Scott Muir as friendly, amusing, and a good raconteur. It was true that he pursued the women with considerable verve, but if another man condemned him for that, was it from a sense of morality or jealousy? He could be generous. Recently, he had paid the air fare of an elderly widow who had wanted to see her family in Australia before she died, but could not afford to do so. Perhaps not quite the character Laura had sketched. Yet she was a better judge of character than he. Steve, an old friend, had come to stay for a week. He'd always found Steve good company, but after he'd left, she had said he was not to be

4

trusted; she'd been annoyed when her judgement had been ridiculed. Some months later, the newspapers had reported Steve's appearance in court on a charge of fraud . . . So was Scott on an ego-trip when he served champagne, not cava, and provided a buffet of which Lucullus would have approved? Locke shrugged his shoulders, drained his glass, and went into the cool indoors.

Two

It was ironic that when they invaded Mallorca, the Moors brought the benefits of religious tolerance, terracing, irrigation, the introduction and production of apricots, almonds, and olives, and when they were thrown out and 'freedom' returned, there was religious intolerance and suffering in the countryside because under the repartiment, the land was divided between the conqueror's followers and the Church, which resulted in wealth for the few and poverty for the many, a situation which lasted for several centuries.

Sa Rotaga, a possessió or landed estate, dated back to the repartiment. Don Maldonado had had the large house built and from it had ruled his property as a tyrant. Fact and fiction had become entwined, but it was generally accepted that one of the feudal peasants had accidentally caused a carriage wheel to be wrecked and Don Maldonado had been so enraged, he had ordered two of his foremen to hold down the unfortunate man whilst he smashed in his head with an iron bar. More open to doubt was another story, that one of the women who worked in the fields – as young and tender as a pea swelling in its pod – had refused his advances; furious that she should reject so great an honour as being deflowered by him, he had said she was to be thrown into one of the two cells the house possessed and she would stay there without food or water until she came to her senses. When she died, her novio had called Don Maldonado a

6

murderer; for his insolence, he had been hanged from a garrover tree . . . Until recently, naughty children had been told that if they did not behave themselves, they would meet Don Maldonado in his carriage drawn by two fighting bulls, fire coming from their nostrils, who trampled anyone in their way . . .

By the beginning of the twenty-first century, the estate had been reduced to no more than eight hectares – one of the previous owners had been an even more compulsive gambler than most Mallorquins – yet the old people still referred to it as a possessió. The present house, built in the middle of the nineteenth century, was three floors high and U-shaped around a courtyard; the tall stone walls and small windows had once imparted a forbidding appearance, but this was almost banished by the gardens which provided colour and beauty throughout the year. In the centre of the courtyard was a large fountain, with carved sides, in which a three-metre jet rose and fell – in the height of the summer, its gentle, tinkling sound provided a soothing aural backdrop. All the water used on the estate came from a well, four metres wide and a hundred deep, which had been dug out by hand; it had never been known to run dry.

Muir had employed an interior designer from Barcelona to furnish and decorate the house and contrary to what might have been expected, considering the esteem in which he was held by fashion critics, his work had proved to be pleasantly attractive.

Muir's parties seldom varied. Champagne in never failing quantity was served by two waiters from one of the restaurants in Llueso; Elena, who was employed full time in the house, oversaw the buffet meal, which in terms of quality, quantity, and variety, could hardly have been surpassed. Most guests remained indoors, since the air-conditioning ensured coolness in which to enjoy the plenitude unknown in their own homes; the younger minority sported in and about the very large swimming pool, hurrying back to the house when glasses or plates were empty – the air was so dry and warm that even though they had just left the pool, by the time they reached the house, they shed very few drops of water.

In the larger of the drawing rooms, Jane said to her husband: 'If you're not careful, your eyes will get locked.'

'What's that supposed to mean?' Reed asked, as he continued to stare at the slender, shapely, notably attractive blonde who was talking to Muir.

'You've been ogling that woman for the past ten minutes.'

'Ogling suggests an amorous interest; mine is purely appreciative.'

'Of what?'

Laura smiled. 'Since there's not a man present who can tear his eyes off her except to have a glass refilled, that hardly needs answering.'

'Don't they ever grow out of it?' Jane asked.

'Only if their imagination begins to rust.'

'I do wonder where he finds them?' Locke said.

'Soho,' Jane snapped.

Reed spoke to Locke. 'It's sad how unchristian a woman can become when she really tries.'

'Sufficiently unchristian to kick you on the shin if you voice any more remarks like that,' Jane said.

'Shall I tell you where he did meet her?'

'If you're prepared to explain how you know.'

'Scott sailed over to St-Tropez on his yacht and was enjoying an evening gin and tonic at anchor when he heard a cry of distress; a woman swimmer was in distress from cramp. Without a moment's hesitation, despite the fact he was wearing a Harvie and Hudson shirt, he dived in and

8

caught her just before she was about to go under for the third time. Naturally, after so heroic a rescue, romance blossomed.'

'Five glasses of champagne and he thinks he's Barbara Cartland's successor.'

'This is only my third glass.'

'If that's what you think, I'm driving home.'

Suddenly, Laura said: 'Oh, my God!'

'What's up?' Locke asked.

'Can't you see who's heading in our direction?'

Adela came to a halt. She was large in build, florid in complexion, and wore a dress that might have suited someone very much younger; a gentle moustache adorned her upper lip. She had lived on the island longer than any other British expatriate and chose to believe this allowed her to interest herself in other people's lives and to criticize anything with which she disagreed. Her voice was deep. 'The customary embarras de richesses.'

'Few guests seem to be embarrassed,' Reed observed.

'One has to be taught to know where good taste ends and bad taste begins.' She drained her glass, signalled to a waiter to have it refilled.

Reed said: 'And you don't think many of us have had that privilege?'

She drank. 'What privilege?' Small beads of champagne remained on the hairs above her lip and she licked them away.

'Of having been taught good taste. For instance, what about the present company?'

'Don't be so bloody silly,' she said, before she raised her glass and drained it.

'Does that mean—'

Jane interrupted her husband. 'Did you go to the concert the other evening?'

'Couldn't be bothered,' Adela replied. 'The woman can't sing.' She looked around the room.

'I thought she had quite a reputation?'

'Undeserved. As I told Felipe, who was supposed to have organized things, he'd made a bad mistake in booking her. I also pointed out how ridiculous it was to charge fifteen euros when most of us aren't made of money, even if he is, thanks to swindling foreigners.' She finally saw a waiter and imperiously beckoned to him.

The waiter eased his way between people and refilled her glass.

'I hear the Patons are leaving the island,' Laura said.

'Who told you that?' Adela was annoyed at not being the first to hear the news.

'Tony.'

'Then it's probably nonsense.'

'He said they're moving to Denia because they find life here on the island too restrictive.'

'They'll be no loss to the community.'

'I don't know. He's helped quite a few people on the quiet.'

'If it was on the quiet, how does anyone know about it? His type always tries to paint a false picture of himself.'

'You don't think most of us are the same?' Reed suggested.

'I am who I appear to be . . . Have you people eaten?'

'Not yet,' Laura answered.

'Then we can all go in together when I've had a touch more champagne . . . Incidentally, I heard something surprising earlier.'

'What was that?' Jane dutifully asked.

'Do you know the Noyes?'

'We've met them.'

'Little people, but reasonably pleasant. Valerie told me

how she'd been down in a shop in the port the previous day and an English couple were having trouble buying what they wanted. She offered to help them – rather ridiculous considering how faulty her Spanish is – and afterwards they asked her if she'd join them for a drink at one of the front bars; she quickly accepted, of course, since they would be paying. This woman told Valerie they were staying at Hotel Cristina and added, very unnecessarily, that her companion wasn't her husband, but a boyfriend. I cannot think why such people believe one is in the least interested in their grubby private lives.' She drank. 'Veuve Clicquot was my father's favourite, not that he could enjoy it very often since service pensions were even more appalling then than they are now. Patriotism has never buttered much bread.'

'You told us you'd heard something surprising,' Reed said.

'And will, if you'll allow me to say anything.'

'My apologies.'

'Valerie said the woman was called Jemima. In my day, that word had an unfortunate meaning and no one with any common sense would have thought of bestowing it on a daughter.'

'Not even though Jemima was the daughter of Job and very attractive?'

'The Bible contains many names one would not wish to bear.'

'I suppose Salome would certainly be inappropriate for some.'

'Shall we go and eat now?' suggested Adela, apparently unaware that she might have been considered when the last sentence was spoken.

'Just before we do, tell us what was so surprising about Jemima.'

11

'She asked Valerie if she knew where her husband lived.'

'She must believe him very broad-minded, since she seems to have brought her boyfriend along.'

'Of course, at first Valerie didn't know who the woman was talking about since she kept calling him Dinty . . .'

'Who?' demanded Locke, so sharply he momentarily attracted the attention of people nearby.

'You know who she was talking about?' Adela called across a waiter and exchanged her empty glass for a full one.

'The name has an echo in the past.'

'You sound as if it has an unpleasant echo. Was it the name of someone who tried to cheat you?'

'Just for once, could you try to mind your own business?'

'Really!' Adela was surprised and outraged.

Reed, embarrassed, tried to move the conversation on. 'So who was Valerie talking about?'

Adela would have liked to stand on her dignity and refuse to answer, but the pleasure of repeating tittle-tattle was not to be denied. 'Not Valerie; Jemima. She was Scott's wife and wanted to know where her husband lived.'

'Are you serious?'

'Don't be absurd. Of course I am.'

'Well I'll be double damned. The old bastard's married. And I've always thought him too smart.'

'The inference could hardly be more pointed,' Jane snapped.

'Au contraire, my sweet. It's just that I've always placed him as a man who'd learned the joys of playing the field without getting his hands tied.' He turned to Adela. 'Has Jemima visited her husband yet?'

'I've no idea,' she replied.

'If she has, I wonder how Tabitha reacted?'

'Who?'

'The latest example of luscious feminine pulchritude to have Scott panting.'

'How do you know her name?' Jane demanded.

'I had a brief chat with her soon after we arrived; brief, because Scott, no doubt fearful my charm would have an effect, intervened.'

'When I was young, we had a cat called Tabitha.'

'Do I detect that that is more than a casual non sequitur?'

Three

Laura and Locke left without eating. With her usual lack of tact, Adela wanted to know what was wrong, was one of them ill?

Fig and almond trees grew in the field in which the cars were parked and as Locke backed, the estate hit the trunk of a fig tree with sufficient force to jolt them. He swore violently.

'For heaven's sake, calm down,' she said.

'Tell me how to do the impossible.'

They turned on to the dirt track, passed an orange grove – the oranges were formed, but still dark green and it was difficult to distinguish them against the leaves – and went through a gateway on to the road.

'It's a coincidence,' she said, as he accelerated fiercely through the gears. 'It has to be. Dinty is a common nickname for people called Muir.'

'How do you know that?'

'I looked up Muir in our dictionary of names.'

'Why?'

'Because . . . because I thought it might somehow help.'

'How could it possibly begin to do that?'

'I wasn't thinking, I was just desperately . . .' She did not finish.

Twelve minutes later, he braked to a halt in front of the

integral garage so that she could get out; he then drove in. Beatriz was in the kitchen and after a formal greeting, spoke quickly to Laura, who had become reasonably fluent in Spanish.

He crossed to the wall cupboard in which glasses were kept. 'Is there a problem?' His Spanish was far less certain than hers and he had understood only the occasional word.

'Someone called about the registration of our well. He needs more details of the pump and will we provide them as soon as possible?'

'They've had the information twice already. Bloody bureaucracy.' There was brief satisfaction in having someone or something to curse. 'What do you want to drink?'

'Nothing after what I've had. And wouldn't it be better if we just ate?'

He brought a glass out of the cupboard, crossed the kitchen, went down into the cellar and poured out a gin and tonic. Adela would have had something very pointed to say, had she seen him – drinking gin after champagne. Was he one of the little people?

In the sitting room, he sat on one of the armchairs. Their dictionary of names, bought when trying to decide what to call their daughter, had listed Zara as meaning, in Arabic, 'brightness of the dawn'. Names could possess the most bitter irony . . .

Years before, he would have described himself as a lucky man. There were no fault lines in the marriage; many would call him wealthy; both Laura and he were in good health; Zara welcomed their relationship even though they were her parents . . . What had there been to remind him of Solon's warning?

The 11th had been a sunny day – he could remember how mocking the sharp sunshine had suddenly become because

15

tragedy belonged to cloud-darkened days. He'd been in the drawing room, looking for a paperback, when the front doorbell sounded. Going through to the hall, he'd met Laura, coming from the kitchen; together, they'd crossed to the front door, which he had opened. A uniform policeman had said: 'Mr Keir Locke?'

The policeman's manner might have warned him, had he not wondered if he'd been guilty of some minor motoring offence and tried to remember what that could be.

Laura, with a mother's instinct, had immediately known fear. 'Has something happened to Zara?'

'I'm very sorry to have to tell you, madam, that a deceased has been found in a flat and there is reason to believe she may be your daughter.'

'Oh, Christ!' she'd whispered. Then she'd shouted: 'No! No! No!'

He'd had to identify the body. Zara had been wheeled into the reception room of the mortuary, rather than being left on a stainless-steel table, to lessen the emotional impact. As if anything could. As he stared down at her dead face, which, thanks to the skills of the pathologist's assistant, appeared merely to be sleeping, he had silently shouted his pain . . .

There was a brief suicide note in which she apologized to her parents for the hurt she knew she would cause them. It was established she had died from a cocktail of medicines, obtainable from any chemist without a prescription, lethal only when combined with each other; the recipe for this poisonous brew had appeared on the Internet.

They had been asked if they could identify 'Dinty'; they had numbly answered they could not and why were they being asked? The detective sergeant had been brusque, perhaps to keep at arm's length the emotional misery he was plumbing; having read the diary, there was cause, he'd told them, to believe her friendship with Dinty had marked her introduction to drugs and naturally they wanted to identify him. With growing anger, they'd assured the detective that Zara would never have taken drugs and the medical findings he quoted had to be incorrect. He had looked at them with weary sadness, touched with contempt, because they thought their lifestyle would have protected their daughter.

He'd read the diary long before Laura could nerve herself to do so. Some entries had brought tears, others wild, impotent anger. Zara had met Dinty at a party given by the firm of solicitors for whom she worked, to mark the partnership's seventy-fifth year. Dinty, a major client, had singled her out and she'd been amused and flattered; amused because he was older than she, flattered because he was handsome, possessed of a sophisticated charm and she was not – in her own eyes – the most attractive woman present.

He'd entertained her royally; he'd tried to bed her on their fifth evening together. No stranger to eager men, she'd still been disturbed by the animal force of his advances and his reaction to her refusal. 'You think Victoria's still on the throne, you pathetic virgin?' he'd shouted, before storming out of her flat.

Two days later, the diary entry read:

> Dinty phoned. I put the phone down. He tried again. I did the same. He tried a third time and shouted mea culpa, mea maximum culpa as I put the receiver to my ear. His apologizing in Latin, which was Double Dutch as far as he was concerned, made me giggle. He said he must see me again or he'd cut his throat. With what? No answer. He promised by all the saints in the calendar and any that had got left out, he wouldn't

try to pull my panties down. I told him that now
he was being pathetically Victorian. Modern ladies
didn't wear panties. It was either nothing or a thong.
'What's a thong? Will you show me?' God, how
corny a man becomes when he's horny!

Further entries only shadowed the facts, yet no one reading them could doubt what had happened. Dinty had used
his wealth and charm to pursue, she had lacked the sharp
experience necessary to understand he was pursuing her
with such intensity because she had denied him and he must
reverse this failure; success was what mattered in life.

They drove in his Ferrari to Ascot, Henley, Glyndebourne,
anywhere that conventional snobbery said it was chic to
be seen; they ate at the smartest restaurants where they
were treated as VIPs by the maître d's, who knew how to
massage egos when it would pay handsomely to do so. He
mentioned he had a little BMW Z3, as well as the Ferrari
and an Audi, and since he never used it, she might as
well borrow it and when she wanted petrol she was to
put it down to his account. On St Valentine's Day, he had
given her a small diamond and ruby brooch – a Victorian
brooch, he'd assured her. They went to parties at which
there were people from the media and the smart world,
famous or infamous; drink flowed and drugging was cool.
At the third of these parties, he'd snorted cocaine and tried
to persuade her to do the same. Her refusal had annoyed
him and he'd ostentatiously begun to show interest in a
blonde artist whose nickname was Seventy because that
was an advance on sixty-nine. A man, three parts drunk,
had come up to her and asked if she was Dinty's little
ingénue?

He hadn't been in touch for a fortnight. It was long
enough for her to discover how much she missed his easy

charm, his carefree attention, and – although it was a couple of pages before she acknowledged this – the pleasure of a hedonistic life. So when he did phone and suggest a meal in a newly opened restaurant where the cooking was reputed to be exceptional, she'd hummed and hawed just long enough to massage her self-respect before accepting. Several days later, they'd gone to a party. He'd snorted cocaine and suggested she find out for herself that most of what was written and spoken about drugs was nonsense. Because she didn't want to antagonize him again, wanted to believe what he said, and Seventy was again present, she'd done as he had suggested. She'd experienced cheerfulness and the strange, exhilarating mental dichotomy of a sense of detachment, yet total clarity . . .

He'd told her he needed a short break and had booked a suite in the Martinez in Cannes for the coming weekend; since there were two bedrooms, her virtue would be unsullied if she chose to go with him. His psychological study of the art of seduction had proved sound – the second bedroom had not been occupied.

Although sufficiently modern to accept an affair as a pleasant interlude and not a commitment, she was at the same time sufficiently old-fashioned because of her background to regard his enthusiasm as evidence he would propose to her. She discovered her mistake soon after returning to England when it became obvious he regarded their relationship as of a temporary nature and now at an end. He had met her pleas and accusations with the same chilling indifference and to her intense mortification had finally realized it had been her resistance which had fuelled his passion, not love. Desperately unhappy, hating herself, unwilling to confide in her family, she'd sought the temporary relief to which he'd introduced her – cocaine.

She was earning a good salary, her parents were giving

her a generous 'dress allowance', but she still did not have enough money to meet the cost of the drugs her body now craved. Her dealer, refusing credit, had offered her a couple of wraps if she opened her legs for him. Disgusted by both suggestion and man, convinced the world would offer only further degradation, she had used the Internet to call up the recipe for death.

She'd bought the various medicines at different chemists for fear that if she didn't, her intention would be obvious – she was no longer thinking clearly. She'd made up the slightly oily, dark green mixture and before drinking it, had written one last entry in her diary. 'What is hell? Hell is oneself.' . . .

As Locke emptied his glass, Laura came into the room. 'Even if . . .' she began, then stopped. She stared at him for several seconds, her expression strained, then slumped down on the nearest chair. 'The detective said the diary entries weren't sufficient legally to prove Dinty had introduced Zara to drugs.'

'Whatever they told us, they were obviously so keen to identify him, they can't have had any doubts.'

'But if it was he and the police identified him, what would they do? It's ages ago and everything will have changed.'

'I don't give a damn what's changed, I'm going to find out if Scott was the Dinty who was responsible for Zara's . . . death.'

'And if he was?'

'I'll tell him precisely what kind of a bastard he is.'

'What good will that do?'

'If there's even a spark of conscience under the self-satisfaction, it'll twitch and hurt.'

'He'll never admit the truth.'

'Of course not. But she met him at the partnership's

seventy-fifth party and they can say whether they had Scott Muir as a client and he was invited.'

'They'll refuse to tell you on the grounds of confidentiality.'

'Confidentiality will become very vague if I say I need to get in touch with him for the benefit of the two of us and hint that if I succeed there might be considerable work for them.'

'Keir, please don't. I'm scared.'

'Of what?'

'You have such a quick temper.'

'It's something I have to do. For her sake.'

And, she wondered, for yours? Although he had never explained why – perhaps couldn't – he had felt responsible for Zara's death. Did he hope finally to shed that responsibility by facing and accusing the guilty man?

Four

Monday was not normally a cheerful day, but this one was proving to be an exception. Superior Chief Salas's secretary had just rung to say he had unexpectedly flown to Madrid and would be there until Thursday, which meant there would be no call for the report until Friday. Since Alvarez hadn't prepared any report and couldn't remember precisely why he should have done, Salas's absence was doubly welcome.

Good fortune induced optimism. Perhaps Dolores was preparing Guatlleres amb figes for lunch. When she cooked quail, she served a miracle of taste. He'd once asked her what was the trigger for this miracle and she had ridiculously replied, a spoonful of bitter chocolate. Women preserved the secrets of cooking as zealously as the secrets of themselves.

He yawned, checked the time and decided that even though Salas was no longer on the island, it would be some time yet before he could reasonably leave the stifling hot office and return home. He stared at the five letters on the desk, left there some time before by the duty cabo, and wondered whether to open them. With nothing better to do, he did so. The first three were unimportant; the fourth contained a request from a fellow inspector to ascertain whether Jacob Ramirez was living in the Port Llueso area and, if so, to take a witness statement from him. Since there clearly was no certainty Ramirez was in the area, any search would likely be laborious and probably prove to be a waste of time and effort. He scrumpled up the letter and threw it into the wastepaper basket. In the fifth envelope was a memorandum which reminded all members of the Cuerpo efficient criminal investigation demanded that full and accurate records were kept. The memorandum joined the request.

He settled back in the chair. When he was home and in the relative cool provided by thick rock walls, he would enjoy an iced brandy . . . His mind drifted. Ice had once been a luxury which only the wealthy could enjoy because of the cost of procuring and storing it. In the winter, the nevaters – ice men – had collected snow and ice high up in the mountains and stored this in rock buildings, partially underground, each with a single opening for loading, and roofs of rushes and tiles. In the summer, the ice and snow had been carried in containers, insulated with rushes or straw, on the backs of mules down to the valleys. It had been very hard work, yet the last snow house had only ceased to be used at the end of the first quarter of the last century, having been made redundant by the newly introduced ice machines. In the second half of the century, ice machines had in turn been made redundant by refrigerators (for a while, often kept in the living room, where one's friends and neighbours could see and admire it). Life seemed to be about replacement – and the older one became, the more unjust that was . . .

He awoke and found to his annoyance that he had slept past the time he could legitimately have left for lunch. He made his way downstairs, along the passage past the duty cabo, and out. It was the middle of the season and the streets were crowded with tourists. It was always difficult to decide in what light to view tourists. Their constant stupidity made extra work for him; much, perhaps most, of the coastline had had its quiet beauty destroyed in order to house and amuse them; despite the natural conservatism of the islanders, old ways were disappearing; property values had risen to such levels that young Mallorquins might well despair they would ever be able to buy a home of their own; the high wages paid in hotels, restaurants, and bars, left few willing to work on the land, so that now, absurdly, vegetables and fruit were imported not only from the Peninsula, but also from foreign countries . . . Yet previously, when the very few tourists had been wealthy, well behaved, and responsible for no changes, many islanders had known the bitter ache of poverty and a future without hope . . .

He reached his car, unlocked the driving door, sat behind the wheel and switched on the fan to try to clear away some of the stifling heat. A couple of years back, he had always been able to park close to the office in the shade; recently, so many sections of various streets had been pedestrianized – to make Llueso appear even more attractive to tourists – that now he had to park well away from the office and usually in the sun . . .

He drove through the narrow, twisting streets, many of them one-way – another irritating change – and reached home, two roads back from the torrente that was invariably bone dry in the summer, occasionally a roaring, dangerous flood in winter.

Jaime, seated at the table in the dining room, muttered a greeting. Alvarez reached inside the sideboard and brought out a glass, poured himself a generous brandy. He opened the ice bucket and found it contained only two half-melted cubes. 'We need more ice.'

Jaime nodded.

He looked at the bead curtain across the kitchen doorway. 'What sort of a mood is she in now?'

'A bit more reasonable than she was.'

'I'll get some more ice, then.'

'Whilst you're about it, ask her if she thought to get another bottle of coñac; this one's almost empty.'

'Didn't you remind her to buy one?'

'Forgot.'

Like hell he'd forgotten, Alvarez decided. Jaime suffered a cowardly reluctance to do or say anything which might annoy Dolores. He had never understood that a husband needed to be master in his own house.

Alvarez picked up the ice bucket and went through the bead curtain into the kitchen, which, despite the upright fan switched on to maximum speed, was stiflingly hot. Dolores's face was beaded with sweat, there was a smudge of flour on her nose, her apron, worn over an old frock, was badly stained, and yet when she straightened up and stared at him, she possessed all the haughty pride of an Andaluce in the finery of La Feria.

'What do you want?' she asked sharply.

Since she could see the ice bucket, the question was unnecessary. Jaime was wrong. Her mood had not improved. So if he were to avoid pointed comments about the need for more ice only because he was drinking too much, he must try to please her. 'It smells as if the meal's going to be even more delicious than usual.'

She began to chop an onion.

'Could it be Guattleres?'

She chopped more vigorously. 'You think that in this heat – not that you will be suffering it since you sit and rest – I am going to slave ever harder in order to serve a meal to men who will have drunk so much they can hardly tell the difference between a crust of dried bread and coranzomes de alcachofas con foi-gras?'

'That's not right—'

'As my mother told me many times, when a man complains something is not right, he is confessing that the truth has escaped.' She picked up a saucepan and angrily swept the chopped onion into it with a sweep of a large-bladed knife.

He decided it was not the moment to ask her if she had remembered to buy another bottle of brandy.

Five

He awoke and stared up at the ceiling, patterned by reflected sunshine coming up through the closed shutters.

'Enrique,' Dolores called from downstairs, 'it is almost twenty to five.'

Pleasure now was the knowledge he could safely extend his siesta since the superior chief was not in Palma.

'I have to leave the house very soon. If you're not down within a couple of minutes, you'll have to get your own tea.'

He sat up, swivelled round on the bed and put his feet on the ground, sweating even though he was wearing only pants and the fan was on. It was a summer of prolonged heat, yet authority still demanded people work normal hours . . .

'One day,' Dolores said, as he walked through the bead curtain into the kitchen, 'you'll take root in bed . . . I've made the coffee and the coca is in the cupboard. Jaime's at work and the two children are with friends, so try to make certain you lock up when you leave.'

'You seem to be in a hurry?'

'As I told you when you were upstairs.' She looked around the kitchen, picked up her handbag, and left through the back door.

He watched her pass the window on her way across the tiny courtyard to the passage which ran the length of the house to the road. He'd remarked on her seeming need to hurry in the hopes she would understand she should have put the coca on the table and poured the coffee before she left. Unfortunately, women seldom responded to subtlety.

A quarter of an hour later, he left the house – having made certain every door and window was secured; a precaution which years before would have been unnecessary – and walked along the pavement to his parked car. He could have walked to the office; indeed, had been advised for the good of his health to do so. Soon, he would follow that advice. When the worst of the heat was over.

Minutes after reaching his office, the phone rang. Resentfully, he opened his eyes, reached out and lifted the receiver.

A man said in Mallorquin, his words initially difficult to understand because of the stressed speed with which he spoke: 'You must get here.'

'Who's speaking?'

'Pablo Ortiz.'

'Where are you?'

'Sa Rotaga. That's up—'

'I know where it is. What's the trouble?'

'I went to skim the swimming pool and found him at the bottom of it.'

'Who have you found?'

'Señor Muir.'

'You've pulled him out and tried to revive him?'

'From the look of him he's been there far too long.'

'You haven't tried to get him out?'

'D'you think I don't know a dead 'un when I see one?'

'At the bottom of a pool? Pull him out. It doesn't matter what you reckon, try to resuscitate him. D'you know how?'

'No.'

'Call the medical centre and tell them to send someone immediately and say what to do in the meantime. I'll be with you as soon as I can.'

He replaced the receiver. Muir was a foreign name; probably British. He stood, mopped his face with a handkerchief, made his way downstairs where he spoke to the duty cabo. 'If anyone wants me, I've been called—'

'To the bar in Club Llueso.'

'To Sa Rotaga, where a man's reported drowned in a swimming pool.'

'A real cool death.'

'Show some respect for the dead.'

'Does that include you?'

The young were becoming ever more mannerless.

In the relatively short time his car had been parked, its interior had reached almost furnace heat. He settled behind the wheel and thought longingly of air-conditioning as he drove rapidly through the narrow streets to the Laraix road. Four kilometres along that, he turned left, at a sign marked Sa Rotaga, on to a dirt track.

As he passed the orange grove, he remembered his father, struggling to support the family on the poor land he owned and farmed, saying oranges were God's gift to the peasant because they were filled with the health too expensive to buy from a doctor . . .

He parked in the turning circle, beyond the fountain and behind another car, crossed to the house. The massive wooden door, striated by time, was in two halves and on the right-hand one was a large wrought-iron knocker. Not knowing who might be in the house, he knocked and waited. After a while, the left-hand door was opened by a woman whom he recognized but could not identify. He introduced himself and waited for her to respond; when she did not, he asked her name. She gave it in a sharp voice, making it clear he had been guilty of bad manners in not knowing who she was. She bore no physical resemblance to Dolores, yet reminded him of her in that her manner lacked the sense of respect he, or any other man, should expect. Despite this suggestion of arrogance, many would have called her attractive. 'Is that the doctor's car?'

'Yes.'

'How long has he been here?'

'Maybe five minutes.'

'What's the quickest way to the swimming pool?'

She didn't answer, turned and walked towards an open doorway and he followed. They passed through a large room, well furnished, and she opened a French window to go out on to a covered patio. 'It's on the other side.' She pointed at the trimmed cupressus hedge.

He crossed the lawn – obviously there was no shortage of water – and went through the gateway in the centre of the hedge. Two men were by the sodden figure, dressed in open-neck shirt, linen trousers, and sandals, lying face upwards near the steps into the shallow end of the pool. The doctor, whom he recognized, was making a superficial examination of the dead man. Ortiz, as he presumed the other to be, stood and watched.

Alvarez came to a halt near them and said a formal 'Good afternoon'. The doctor looked up briefly, nodded, resumed his work; Ortiz muttered a couple of words that might have returned the greeting.

The doctor stood. 'Is there hot water in there?' he asked, indicating the large pool complex.

'All you want in either bathroom,' Ortiz replied.

The doctor went into the large glass-fronted central room through the open doorway.

'Does Señor Muir own this property?' Alvarez asked.

'He did,' was the ironic reply.

30

'Was he married?'

'No.'

'Lived here on his own?'

'When he couldn't find a woman.'

'Was there one here last night?'

'No.'

Ortiz's manner made it clear he had had little respect and no liking for his late employer.

The doctor returned.

'Is it confirmed death was due to drowning?' Alvarez asked.

'The fine froth, tinged with blood, in nostrils and mouth are a classic symptom. There can't be much doubt, but you'll need the PM for definite confirmation.'

'Can you say how long he's been dead?'

'Very difficult due to the heat and length of immersion . . . There's still slight rigor, the skin of the feet and hands is markedly wrinkled, and discoloration is beginning at the root of the neck. As a working figure, say between six on Saturday afternoon and five on Sunday morning.'

'That's a pretty wide gap.'

'Impossible to be any more precise.'

'I can tell you he was alive just after five on Saturday afternoon,' Ortiz said.

'You would like to confirm the time of death I have just given?' said the doctor, in tones of annoyance.

Experts never liked to be helped. 'Is there anything to suggest why he drowned?' Alvarez asked.

'Because he had water in his lungs.'

Experts seldom missed the chance to sneer at the layman. 'What I meant was, are there any signs to suggest why he fell into the pool?'

'You can already say with certainty that he fell?'

'I don't think he would have gone for a swim in his clothes.'

'You have a stronger belief in man's essential sanity that I.'

Alvarez hoped that should he need medical attention, it would not be this doctor who gave it. 'Are there any signs of injury?'

'None my examination has uncovered; the far more detailed one at the PM will be necessary for a definitive answer.'

'Then it's probable he was walking by the pool, suffered a heart attack, and fell in?'

'The gardener provides the time of death and you the cause? I need not have bothered to come here.' The doctor picked up his leather medical case and, with short, jerky strides, crossed to the gateway in the hedge and went through.

'Prickly little bastard,' Ortiz said.

Alvarez agreed. 'Is there a phone down here?'

Ortiz nodded.

'Then I'll use it to arrange removal of the body. And afterwards I'll need to ask you one or two questions.'

Alvarez went into the main room of the pool complex and across to the small bar, on which was a phone. He dialled and as he waited for the connexion to be made, studied the bottles on the three shelves against the wall. There were, amongst all the others, one of Hennessey X.O. and two of Bisquit Dubouche. The rich lived richly . . . His call was answered and he arranged for the immediate collection of the body to be taken for a post-mortem.

He called Ortiz inside and they sat on opposite sides of one of the four glass-topped tables. He offered cigarettes.

'Don't smoke. And don't drink.'

Which explained the other's dour character. 'Have you worked here for long?'

'A couple of years.'

'As far as you know, was the señor healthy?'

'Seemed so.'

'You never heard him complain of breathlessness or chest pains?'

'He was forever complaining about something, but not that.'

'A difficult man?'

Given the opportunity to express an opinion, Ortiz suddenly became loquacious. 'Never satisfied. And wouldn't listen to what you said. He wanted a new rose bed, and as I told him, that's something best left to late autumn, when there's been enough rain to soften the ground until it's possible to work it. But when he said he wanted it now, now it had to be. So I've been struggling to install irrigation pipes in soil like concrete and what did he do? Complained it was taking too long.'

'You told the doctor Señor Muir was alive after five Saturday afternoon. How long after?'

'Can't rightly say. Could have been ten minutes, maybe a bit more.'

'Where was he?'

'Here.'

'Then you work on Saturdays?'

'Not usually, but with him complaining, I had to stay on for the afternoon.'

'And you actually saw him then?'

'Would I know he was alive if I didn't?'

'You might have heard, but not seen him.'

'We both saw him.'

'Who's both?'

'Me and Elena, of course.'

'Tell me what happened.'

'We saw him . . .'

'Exactly where and under what circumstances?'

'It's like this. I've been bringing Elena here and taking her home on account of her car being at the garage. She came out and said she had to get home fast and I said OK. So we're about to drive away when the señor comes out of the house and I thought maybe he wants something. So I shout out if he does and he shakes his head. Elena says to drive on because she's in a hurry, so we left.'

Alvarez stubbed out the cigarette. He brought a handkerchief out of his pocket and mopped his forehead, face, and neck. 'It's getting hotter every day.'

'And will do until St Bernard comes and puts out the fires.'

He lit another cigarette.

'Them things kill you,' Ortiz said.

Everything which made life bearable was dangerous. 'When did you get here this morning?'

'Eight, same as always.'

'Were you surprised not to see the señor?'

'If he was with a woman, sometimes he didn't appear until the afternoon was as worn out as him.'

'But he didn't have a guest, you said.'

'Didn't know that until merienda and Elena asked if I'd stayed over.'

'Why might you have done?'

'There's things in the house supposed to be worth more money than you or me'll ever see and the insurance wants someone in there all the time. So when the señor was away, I had to spend the night in the house. She wouldn't because her Lorenzo said she wasn't going to be in the house on her own; never met a man so jealous as Lorenzo. The señor wasn't going to rush back to bed the likes of her; wanted

34

'em young and luscious . . . He paid me extra, of course, but not as much as he should have.'

'Did you wonder why he hadn't asked you to sleep in the house if he was away?'

'Can't say I did.'

'You've been telling me he liked the women?'

'If you had his money, wouldn't you?' He spoke freely, unaware that the enthusiasm with which he recounted what he'd seen made it obvious he did not favour self-denial in all things. The señor had chased the women like a dog after a bitch on heat; being foreign, the women had been eager to be caught. He couldn't guess how many times he'd seen one by or in the pool, bare-titted. And sometimes bare-arsed as well. There was one who'd had a body to make a priest throw aside his soutane . . .

'How did you learn all this?'

It seemed there was a very small hole in the hedge around the pool, not discernible from inside, which allowed a man to see what was going on.

A space kept carefully trimmed, Alvarez guessed. Had the señor never wondered why Ortiz's work suffered when he was with a woman by the pool . . . ?

Three men, one of them carrying a rolled-up body bag, came through the gateway. He met them, confirmed the dead man was to be taken to the mortuary and kept there until the post-mortem. They unrolled the bag, lifted the body on to it, zipped up the bag and carried it away.

Ortiz looked at his watch. 'It's getting on and the wife becomes sharp if I'm not at home when the meal's ready.'

'You'd better be on your way, then, unless you're running Elena home?'

'Which I am.'

'I'll have a quick word with her before you leave.'

'Why?'

'Because that's necessary.'

Ortiz closed and locked the door of the pool house and they made their way to the house. Elena, clearly impatient, was in the kitchen.

'I'll not keep you for long,' Alvarez assured her.

'That's right, you won't. Not with Lorenzo waiting.'

'Lorenzo is your husband . . .'

'You like to imagine I would live with a man who was not my husband?'

'Of course not,' he said hastily. She was of the last generation to value marital chastity more highly than diamonds. 'He might, though, have been your brother . . .'

'I do not have a brother.'

The comparison he had drawn between Dolores and her had been more apt than he had initially recognized. 'What I'm trying to say is, I need a brief word with you, so would you like to telephone your husband and explain you may be a little delayed?'

'I will not be delayed long enough for that.'

'Suppose we sit down . . .'

'There's no call to do so.'

'It'll be more comfortable.'

She looked as if about to argue further, but finally sat.

'I want you to tell me about this morning. You were driven here by Pablo and then what?'

They'd arrived at eight. She'd been surprised to find the kitchen clean . . .

'Why was that?'

'It is not obvious?'

'If you would just explain,' he said meekly.

The señor hadn't said he'd be away, but if he had been at home, she would have expected the kitchen to be in a mess with dirty crockery and cutlery left anywhere and

36

everywhere. He could never be bothered even to stack the dirty things in the dishwasher. Like all men, he had been lazy.

'Did you think that he'd gone away for the weekend?' Alvarez asked.

'Perhaps. But he hadn't asked Lorenzo to stay here.'

'So what did you do?'

'What I always do when I arrive. Clear the kitchen – only there wasn't anything to clear – and then used the house phone to ask what he wanted for breakfast.' She paused. 'And was it for one or two persons?' The words were encased in icy disapproval. 'There was no answer, so I tried again, then went upstairs and banged on the door of his bedroom. Three times. In the end, I opened the door and looked inside.'

No doubt fearful of seeing something that would offend the chastity of her mind.

'What did you see?'

'The bed had not been slept in.'

'Did that worry you?'

'No.'

'Why not?'

'I presumed he had gone away, but had been so disturbed he'd forgotten to ask Lorenzo to be in the house for the night.'

'Why might he have been disturbed?'

She stared at him with contempt. 'What always reduces a man's mind to stupidity?'

'You thought he was off with a woman?'

'Of course.'

'Why did you think that?'

'Did he not have one here on Saturday?'

'And what a woman!' Ortiz said.

'A puta.'

'What a puta!'

'Tell me about her,' Alvarez said.

'What is there to tell? He told me he was having a friend to lunch and wanted me to prepare a special meal.'

'So what did you cook?'

'I suggested Entrecote amb albercocos.'

Alvarez almost tasted the sauce which, thanks to the sun-dried apricots, could make even poor-quality meat a truly notable dish. 'I'll bet he said, yes, please.'

'Then you are a poor gambler. The señor seldom said please or thank you and he told me his woman would prefer something better, so I was to cook boeuf en croûte. A French meal better than a Spanish meal!'

'Nevertheless, very tasty.'

'So you too would choose that?'

'When you're doing the cooking, I'm quite sure either would be culinary heaven . . . Did they enjoy the meal?'

'The señor, always difficult with a woman around, told me in his terrible Spanish that his puta had not eaten much because the meat should have been cooked longer. As if she knew anything except how to ply her trade!'

'What happened after they'd finished the meal?'

'They went upstairs.'

'For fun and games, presumably?'

'I presume nothing since I do not concern myself with matters no decent woman ever does.'

'I'll tell you one thing,' Ortiz said, 'he didn't ring the bells as loudly as he wanted.'

'Why d'you say that?' Alvarez asked.

'He wouldn't drive her back to the Hotel Terramar, but made me do that. And was he in a bloody bad temper when he told me!'

'When was this?'

'Middle, late afternoon.'

'So you took her down to the port, dropped her, and returned here?'

'That's right.'

'Did she talk to you on the journey, say anything which explained why he was so bad tempered?'

'She couldn't speak Spanish and I don't know any English. But the way she kept smiling made me . . . I tell you, if I hadn't been a married man . . .'

'You would still have had ridiculous thoughts,' Elena snapped. 'As if she would ever favour you!'

'Why shouldn't she?'

'Consult a mirror.'

'There's a lot of women would be happy for me to take an interest in them.'

'Only if you paid enough.'

Alvarez spoke hurriedly, to prevent further annoyance. 'I've asked all the questions I need to for the moment, so you can leave when you want.'

She hesitated. 'I don't rightly know . . . With him dead, oughtn't there to be someone here?'

'I'm not staying,' Ortiz said.

'In the circumstances, I don't think anyone can be expected to be here,' Alvarez said. 'We'll just hope no one considers breaking in before we can find out what's going to happen to the estate.'

Since his words accorded with their wishes, they accepted them and left.

Six

Alvarez adjusted the fan in an effort to gain more benefit from its draught, slumped back in the chair, stared at the telephone and reflected how much easier life must have been before Alexander Bell. Then, even a few kilometres had distanced one from a superior, orders had taken so long to arrive that there was no longer good reason to carry them out; requests from fellow officers became so out-of-date they were best ignored; a man could lead a peaceful life, not one of rush, tension, impossible demands . . .

It was finally merienda time. He went downstairs and out into the street, made his way to Club Llueso. The barman poured him a coffee and a brandy without being asked and he carried cup, saucer, and glass over to one of the window tables. Once seated, he stared out at the moving crowd. A young, attractive woman, blonde hair falling almost to her shoulders, went past. The barman, collecting empty cups and saucers at the next table, spoke to Alvarez. 'You're looking even more dismal than usual.'

'Because I've realized the perversity of life. Temptation is only offered to someone who can't take advantage of it.'

'Is that supposed to mean something? If I didn't know you, I'd say you were suffering from overwork.'

'Suppose you do a little work and pour me another coñac?'

'Before you've finished the one in front of you?'

'A problem soon resolved.'

The barman moved on. Alvarez drank some coffee, some brandy, poured the rest of the brandy into the remaining coffee. When he returned to the office, he was going to have to phone Salas . . . He suddenly remembered a fact that had escaped him until then – Salas was in Madrid and would remain there until Thursday. 'Make that a large brandy,' he called out.

'Some day, surprise me.' The barman went behind the bar and put into the sink the glasses, cups, saucers, and teaspoons he'd collected.

Twenty-five minutes later, Alvarez returned to the post, climbed the stairs – slowly, since to hurry in the heat was a grave health risk – and gratefully sat. He stared at the telephone, lifted the receiver, dialled.

'Superior chief's office,' said his secretary, as always sounding as if she had a plum in her mouth.

'Inspector Alvarez speaking.'

'What do you want?' Her manner, moulded on Salas's, was curt.

'I have to report an accidental drowning . . .'

'You have forgotten the superior chief is in Madrid?'

'I reckon the matter isn't sufficiently important to bother him in Madrid, so thought if I mentioned it to you, the next time you're in touch, you can tell him . . .'

'The superior chief requires all reports to be given to him personally.'

'Yes, but—'

'Further, they are to be made at the first possible moment.'

'But when it's not important . . .'

'Do you have the number?'

'Of what?'

'The superior chief's mobile,' she answered in long-suffering tones.

'It's somewhere around, but just for the moment . . .'

'Six four six—'

'Hang on. I need to find a pencil to write the number down.' He didn't doubt she always had one to hand; probably two, in case a lead broke. 'OK, go ahead.'

Having given the full number, she cut the connexion in the middle of his thanks and without bothering to say goodbye. It was how the superior chief would have ended the conversation.

He drummed his fingers on the desk, could think of no acceptable reason not to phone Salas, dialled. The phone rang six times before Salas said, his anger very evident: 'What the devil is it?'

'Inspector Alvarez speaking, Señor—'

'Who else would phone me in the middle of a very important address, forcing me to leave the conference hall!'

'I'm afraid I didn't know—'

'Why are you phoning me?'

'To report that an Englishman who lived in Sa Rotaga – that's up the Laraix valley – has drowned in his swimming pool and—'

'What are the suspicious circumstances surrounding his death?'

'There aren't any.'

'What do you mean?'

'It looks as if he had a heart attack when by the pool, fell in, and drowned.'

'Are you confessing you have called me on my mobile, causing it to disturb and annoy the lecturer to the extent I was forced to leave the hall, merely to report an accidental drowning?'

'Señor, as I have been reminded, you have recently complained that all reports have been taking far too long to reach you and so they must be made at the earliest possible moment—'

'Most people would have the intelligence to understand my order referred to matters of importance. The accidental drowning of an Englishman is of no importance whatsoever.'

'But your order did say—'

'A written order does not speak.'

'What I'm trying to point out is—'

'Probably unclear even to yourself.'

'It was your secretary who told me to ring you in Madrid.'

'She said you were to do so?'

'I suppose not specifically. But when she gave me your mobile telephone number—'

'Only because bitter experience has not yet taught her the danger of leaving anything to your judgement.'

'I did say the matter wasn't important and could be left, but I thought perhaps she'd still mention it to you, in which case, there was the possibility you might be worried it was a serious case even though I didn't get in direct touch with you and tell you what the problem was . . .'

'I am seldom concerned about what you do not tell me, all too frequently by what you do . . . Let me now explain matters in the simplest possible terms. You will not bother me again when I am in Madrid unless a revolution breaks out. Is that clear?'

'Yes, Señor.'

Salas switched off his mobile.

On Thursday morning, the southerly wind brought a fine dusting of Saharan sand and raised temperatures to 41. In his office, Alvarez day-dreamed of glaciers, snow, and a frosted glass in which several ice cubes jostled each other amongst the brandy . . .

The phone rang.

'Manuel Pascual, Institute of Forensic Pathology. We've completed the post-mortem of Scott Muir and confirm he died of drowning in fresh water. As to the time of death, we cannot be any more precise than the doctor.'

'Then that wraps everything up,' Alvarez said gratefully.

'Not so fast.'

'How's that?' he asked, suddenly uneasy.

'While the cause of death is clear, events leading up to that certainly aren't.'

'But the doctor who examined him said there was nothing to suggest he'd suffered from anything other than drowning.'

'Since there were all the classical symptoms, the cause of actual death was clear and with no immediately visible signs to suggest trauma – the fibres of the shirt had swollen to conceal the very small points of entry, the colour of the shirt hid what signs of external bleeding, which was very much less than the internal bleeding, had not been washed away during the long immersion – it is hardly surprising he saw no need for the detailed examination of the naked torso which would have revealed the two puncture marks.'

'What puncture marks?'

'On the right-hand side, just above the hip, are two small wounds, roughly one and a half centimetres apart. The instrument which caused these did not penetrate deeply enough to damage any vital organ and normally would not have been serious. But the deceased suffered from a complaint in which the mechanisms that normally stem a flow of blood after a wound, fail to do so. That's something which can be occasioned by old age, an immunological effect on the lining of the blood vessels, a vitamin C deficiency, as well as several other causes.'

It was not a complaint of which Alvarez had previously heard. For a moment, he wondered if he was unknowingly suffering from vitamin C deficiency and what, in this context, 'old age' meant?

His morbid questions were brought to an end when Pascual resumed speaking.

'The small blood vessel which was ruptured by the left-hand wound failed to heal itself and there was a gradual loss of blood. As this continued, it first became serious, then fatal. Muir will have suffered a growing weakness and then disorientation, which one can assume is why he fell into the swimming pool.'

'How long after the wounds would he have died?'

'Very difficult to assess. The best estimate we can offer is between one and two hours.'

'But the wounds killed him?'

'He died as a result of them.'

'And he was stabbed?'

'There has to be the possibility he fell on to something which inflicted the wounds. As far as we can judge, the instrument, made of metal, was thin, perhaps one millimetre, and widened to four millimetres; it was curved.'

'So the most likely answer is, stabbing?'

'Yes.'

'What was the weapon?'

'I've just described its probable characteristics and to date no one can suggest what these fit.'

'Could we be talking about some form of stiletto?'

'We've no record of one of such shape.'

'A hypodermic needle?'

'As used on an elephant? Such needles don't broaden out and aren't curved.'

'You can't suggest anything?'

'At the moment, that's right.'

Pascual, Alvarez noted, had made the admission easily since from now on it would not be his laborious task to try to identify the instrument of death.

'Were the two wounds inflicted at the same time or in sequence?'

'Impossible to answer.'

'What about falling on the tines of a rake?'

'Back to the problem of the widening curve, though I suppose some rakes do curve. But there were no signs of surrounding bruising and no foreign substances impacted into the wounds; if he'd fallen on to something used in the garden, or house for that matter, we would expect to have found some form of foreign substance in the wounds. They were perfectly clean.'

'So it's probably back to stabbing with a weapon of unknown type?'

'Correct.'

Minutes later, the call ended. Alvarez silently swore. A murder case was difficult enough when one knew what type of weapon had been used, but when it seemed that it had been of an unknown character . . . He reached down to the right-hand drawer of his desk and brought from it a glass and a bottle of Soberano. He had finished his first drink and was about to pour a second one when the phone rang. Since it was too early for him legitimately to have left the office, he answered the call.

'Where is your full report?' Salas demanded.

'On what, Señor?'

'The accidental drowning.'

46

'I was waiting to deliver it after you arrived back from Madrid.'

'Due to unforeseen circumstances, I returned early this morning.'

'As a matter of fact, Señor, it is an advantage that I hadn't submitted my report.'

'An advantage to whom? You?'

'Had I done so, it would have been incorrect.'

'Where you are concerned, that is always a probability.'

'A potter cannot make a pot without clay; a judge must know all the facts if he is to make a true judgement.'

'Are you drunk?'

'Señor, had I made my report earlier, it would have been without the evidence from the post-mortem and that is why you have not yet had it.'

'Were you not only a moment ago suggesting you had not delivered it because you believed me still to be in Madrid?'

'It is a combination of—'

'Incompetence and laziness. What are the results of the PM?'

'As far as the facts can be ascertained, Señor Muir actually died from drowning. But he was suffering from an unusual complaint which prevents the blood clotting – at least I take it that is what is meant by saying the mechanisms which normally stem a flow of blood after a wound fail to do so—'

'Wound?'

'Two.'

'Why has there been no mention of these before?'

'Because they were so fine and the water had dispersed any external bleeding, they weren't noticed until the PM. Had he not been suffering from this complaint

– apparently caused by old age, a lack of vitamin C, and other causes . . . It's very unsettling to learn what can happen . . .'

'Is it too much to ask what did happen?'

'The two puncture wounds were on the right-hand side, above the hip. A blood vessel was ruptured and because the bleeding was not stemmed, he became weaker and weaker and eventually so disorientated, he fell into the pool and drowned. Even though the wounds would not normally have resulted in his death, the fact he died as a direct result of them must mean that legally—'

'You are a qualified lawyer?'

'No, Señor '

'Then keep to what you do know, however limiting you find that. You are saying he was stabbed and so this is a case of murder?'

'Doesn't that rather depend on the legal definition of the facts?'

'Was he stabbed?' demanded Salas, louder than necessary.

'There is the alternative, that he accidentally fell on to something with thin, curved points . . .'

'Is there anything in the home or garden on to which he might have fallen and suffered the injuries?'

'I haven't had time to check because I've only just learned about the wounds.'

'I don't suppose it occurred to you to ask for an opinion as to what kind of weapon might have been used if it was not an accident?'

'The nature of the wounds makes it very difficult for him to describe a possible weapon; in fact, he said he couldn't. It's thin, broadens out, and is curved. I suggested a stiletto, but as he said, who has seen a curved stiletto? A hypodermic needle was another possibility, but he said it would have to be for an elephant and once again, would not be curved—'

'I don't think you need list all your impossible suggestions. You do realize what has happened, don't you?'

'Yes, Señor. As I have been saying—'

'You first report to me, at the most inappropriate moment, an accidental drowning and then, a mere two days later, the case becomes murder by stabbing.'

'Until the PM results came through, there was no suggestion of anything but drowning.'

'An efficient officer regards every possibility as feasible until it can be eliminated.'

'But when the doctor said all the visible signs pointed to death by drowning, it seemed he must have fallen into the water after a heart attack—'

'You had reason to believe he suffered from heart problems?'

'I thought it feasible to do so since at that time I could not eliminate the possibility.'

'You mistake insolence for respectful understanding.'

There was a long silence.

'What was the motive for his murder?' Salas asked.

'I can't yet say.'

'Who can be considered a suspect?'

'I don't yet know.'

'It would seem you have still to begin an investigation.'

'I received the report from the Institute only minutes before you phoned me.'

'Time enough to start. An ambitious officer uses each minute as if it were an hour.'

That must make for a hell of a long working day.

'Was Señor Muir wealthy?'

'Judging by his home, very wealthy.'

'Then the motive will almost certainly be money.'

'Or sex.' The moment he'd spoken, Alvarez regretted his words. Salas was a prude.

'I had wrongly imagined this to be a case which could give you no scope for your very unfortunate interest in that subject. I failed to allow for the enthusiasm of your perverted imagination.'

'But sex is at the bottom of so many crimes . . . Perhaps, Señor, I should rephrase that. Sex is the motive for so many crimes and Señor Muir was entertaining ladies all the time—'

'It does not occur to you that a man and a woman may enjoy a platonic friendship because they are normal, cultivated persons?'

'I don't know how cultivated he was, but he was certainly normal. Apparently, when he and one of his recent women were down by the pool, they were naked and doing what one would consider normal in such circumstances—'

Salas cut the connexion.

Since the superior chief was unlikely to phone again, Alvarez decided there was no practical reason to prevent his returning home soon and enjoying an iced brandy; or two.

Seven

Alvarez awoke and enjoyed several moments of dreamy reflection before he left the bed. In the kitchen, Dolores served him a cup of hot coffee and two large slices of coca. It was a pleasant start to the evening.

He drove up the Laraix valley, turned off on to the track leading to Sa Rotaga. Who, he wondered as he passed the orange grove, would be the next owner of the estate? Someone who possessed sufficient soul to know the house and such land as remained should be preserved as a link with the past? Much more likely, it would be turned into a luxury hotel and those who stayed there would not give a damn who Don Maldonado had been, would not hear the faint cries of the imprisoned maiden, would not look at the garrover tree and shiver . . .

He parked, crossed to the steps, opened the heavy right-hand door, stepped inside and called out. A moment later, Elena appeared, apron in one hand.

'I've come to have a word with you and Pablo,' he said.

'You can speak to him, but not to me,' she answered curtly.

'Why is that?'

'I need to be home to prepare Lorenzo's meal.'

'It's important I talk to you—'

'Not so important as seeing he has something good to

51

eat. When a man works hard all day, he needs a proper meal in the evening.'

'I wouldn't argue with that.'

'Looking at you, that is very obvious. If you wanted to talk to me, you should have arrived sooner.'

'I have been very busy.'

'And, no doubt, think you are the only one! The señor, the Good Lord look after him, is dead, but that does not mean I forget my job and leave the house to collect dust.'

'Of course not.'

'I have spent all day cleaning and polishing. So before I leave, you will tell me this. Who will now pay me and Pablo for our work?'

'Someone will have to talk to the señor's heir, whoever that is, before you can be answered. In the meantime—'

'I will continue to keep the house clean and tidy.'

He silently praised her sense of loyalty. If the new owner had a gram of common sense, he or she would try to make certain Elena continued to work in Sa Rotaga . . . 'I'll have a word with you tomorrow, then.'

'As you please.'

'Presumably, Pablo will be leaving with you?'

'I cannot say.'

'Won't he be driving you home?'

'I have my car once more. And a bill which says the mechanic will be dining on turbot.'

'There is one thing.'

'I'm in a hurry.'

'It won't take a second. Where were you Saturday afternoon after you left here?'

'Where should you think? I was at home.'

'And you were there all evening and night?'

'With a man to look after, am I likely to have spent time doing what I wanted?'

'So Lorenzo will be able to say you were at home right through until Sunday.'

'Why do you ask these questions?'

'To confirm you were not here . . . When you last saw the señor, did he say or do anything to make you think he was in any way disturbed?'

'Nothing.'

'Then that's all I have to ask for now . . . By the way, I'll be having a word with Lorenzo to ask him to confirm what you've just told me.'

'You believe me to be a liar?'

'Of course not. But the rules say I must . . . Just before you leave, can you tell me where Pablo is likely to be?'

'Wherever there is least work to do.'

He thanked her for her help and made his way through the house to the garden. She had possibly been more correct than she had really believed. Ortiz had settled on one of the chairs in the pool house.

'Been working until I needed a bit of a rest,' Ortiz explained.

'The man who sometimes rests, lives to see his grand-children.' Alvarez settled in another chair. 'I need to ask some questions, the first of which is, can you think of anything here or in the grounds that has two, maybe more, sharp, curved points sticking out?'

'Why are you asking?'

'The señor died from drowning, right enough, but the post-mortem shows he fell into the pool because he'd lost so much blood internally, following a couple of wounds to his side. I have to determine whether he was accidentally injured.'

'There wasn't no signs of wounds when I hauled him out.'

'They were small, too inconspicuous to be readily

53

noticed, and normally would not have caused his death, but he suffered from blood that wouldn't clot and so he bled internally until he became weak and disorientated, fell into the pool, and didn't have the energy to save himself.'

'It's a funny way to go.'

'Whatever caused the wounds was probably metal, very pointed, and curved. If it was something he ran into or fell on to, it had at least two tines. Can you suggest anything, anywhere, which fits the description, on a wall, on the ground?'

Ortiz was silent as he stared into the distance. Finally, he said: 'There ain't nothing I know about.'

'Then I'll have to have a wander about the place and see if I can find something.'

'I'll not stop you, but you won't find anything.'

'I don't suppose I will. But the negative will be just as important as the positive.'

'How's that?'

'If there's nothing, then it's likely he wasn't accidentally injured.'

'You're suggesting someone did him in?'

'It's possible . . . If I ask you if you can name someone who might have really disliked him, what is your answer?'

'I'd say, I can't name 'em, but there must have been a whole tribe. Women, like as not.'

Alvarez stared out at the pool. 'This weather makes a man thirsty,' he said reflectively. 'The señor's not going to do any more drinking and I was always taught that if you don't eat and drink what's offered today, you'll go hungry and thirsty tomorrow. So how about having something from one of the bottles on the shelves behind the bar?'

'I don't drink.'

He had forgotten. He stood, crossed to the bar, found

54

a glass in one of the small cupboards, poured himself a Bisquit, a mark he had not previous tasted. He hesitated before adding ice, but decided the heat made convention of lesser account. He returned to the chair, sat. 'Tell me about Saturday.'

'I said.'

'Tell me again. You were working on a new rose bed?'

'It was stupid with the ground rock-solid. Didn't listen. Never did.'

'Perhaps it was more that he didn't understand much Spanish?'

'If he'd talked it better than you or me, he wouldn't have listened. He wanted his rose bed and so I had to bust a gut giving it to him.'

'He always insisted on having his own way?'

'And if we tried to say it was a bloody stupid way, he treated us like we was nobody because he paid our wages.'

'What sort of a mood was he in on Saturday?'

'Didn't see much of him after he said I was to carry on with the rose bed – he was busy, wasn't he? Then after lunch he told me I was to drive his woman to the port and he was in as black a mood as I've ever seen.'

'Any idea what upset him?'

'His woman, of course. She must have kept her legs crossed.'

'Was she equally upset?'

'Not her. Smiling, cheerful . . . To tell the truth, when I was taking her back to the hotel, she was acting like she wouldn't mind me having a stab.'

'Did you?'

'With the wife waiting at home?' Then in a moment of honesty, he said: 'Anyway, likely I was imagining. Her kind don't waste themselves on the likes of me; money, that's what gets 'em excited.'

'So you reckon he wasn't wealthy enough to excite her?'

'Why d'you say that?'

'According to you, he was so angry because she wouldn't come across.'

'Yes, well . . .' Ortiz said meaninglessly.

'Where did you drive her?'

'The Hotel Terramar. I said before.'

'And then you returned here?'

'Had to, seeing I'd used his car and there was time to go before I finished work.'

'What happened when you did finish?'

'Elena came and found me and said it was time to go home, so we left.'

'You both saw the señor before you left?'

'We were in my car when he came out of the house. I thought he looked like he wanted something and called out to ask, but he shook his head; Elena told me to drive on because she was in a hurry. She can be real sharp.'

'So I've noticed. When you say you thought he wanted something, could he have been trying to get your help?'

'He'd have said so, wouldn't he, instead of just shaking his head?'

'So he was uninjured at that time?'

'Isn't that what I keep telling you?'

'Was the señor on his own when you left?'

'Yes.'

'Have you any idea whether he was expecting a visitor?'

'Can't say whether he knew about the señor; Elena can maybe tell you.'

'What señor?'

'We passed his car by the oranges, which took a bit of doing because the track's narrow there . . . I told Señor Muir more than once it needed widening at that point, but he said it would cost too much when two vehicles only met very occasionally. Funny thing about the rich – they guard the euros more closely than you and me.'

'That's how they stay rich. Do you know who the other man was?'

'I didn't get too good a look, considering I was avoiding the car – but Elena must have done because she said what nice people he and his wife were.'

Alvarez drained his glass. 'I'll have a wander in a minute. Maybe after another little drink.'

'You won't find nothing like you described.'

'I accept what you say, but my superior chief is bound to ask me if I've made a thorough search. Which reminds me, I'll need a word with your wife.'

'Why?'

'So she can confirm you were at home Saturday night and Sunday morning.'

'I suppose now you're going to tell me you believe me and wouldn't bother with asking her but for your boss?'

'That's right.'

'What would you do if I said I reckon you're a bloody liar?'

'I'd go and pour that drink,' Alvarez answered, as he stood.

Eight

Alvarez searched the pool complex and garden and found nothing which could possibly have inflicted the wounds suffered by Muir. Sweating, tired, breathless, he made his way to the house and as he entered, heard banging on the front door. He went through to the hall and opened the left-hand half of the door to face a man and a woman. The man's shaven head, heavily featured face with scarred cheek, and coarse mouth matched the aggressive tone of his words. 'I've been bloody knocking for hours. I suppose like the rest of you lazy sods on this crummy island, you were fast asleep.'

'Please, Larry, be calm.' The lines on her face and the slight sag of flesh here and there, marked a woman considerably older than her companion; the excessive make-up and the clothes she wore indicated she was doing all she could to suppress that truth.

'I'm sorry,' Alvarez said in English, 'but I didn't hear you earlier because I was in the garden.'

She was plainly disconcerted to realize he'd understood what had been said. 'It's just . . . Well, we've been waiting rather a long time—'

'A bloody long time,' interrupted Grant.

'But it's all right now, Larry.'

'Yeah?'

'We can ask this gentleman—'

'Then why don't you ask him?'

She faced Alvarez. 'We want to speak to someone who can tell us what's happening.'

'With reference to what?'

'Everything. I mean, this house and what's in it.'

'Why should that concern you?'

'Mind you own goddamn business,' shouted Grant.

'I would advise you, Señor—'

'Look, mate, I don't take no advice from a manservant.'

'I am Inspector Alvarez of the Cuerpo General de Policia.'

'Oh, my God! You're some kind of policeman,' she said with nervous alarm. 'Larry didn't understand. It's just that we don't know what to do and Larry's been getting impatient because no one seems to be able to tell us—'

Grant, determined to show he was unimpressed by authority, said with loud belligerence: 'Because they're all as dumb as a dead mule.'

'Please, Larry, don't talk like that,' she pleaded. She spoke to Alvarez once more. 'It's because I've just read about Scott's death in a paper that was in the hotel.'

'You are referring to Señor Muir?'

'Yes.'

'And his death concerns you?'

'I'm his wife.'

'Not much of a policeman since you didn't know that,' sneered Grant.

'Larry, please don't go on. You know what that man in the hotel was saying about the police here.'

Alvarez said: 'Señora, let me assure you that we have become so used to the ways of foreigners, we only shoot someone who is unusually rude.' Their expressions told him they were uncertain whether he had been joking. His

59

manner became more official. 'If you will come into the house, we can discuss the matter and I will give you what help I can.'

She nervously moved past him into the hall; Grant, shoulders very squared, trying to give the impression of contemptuous self-confidence, followed her. Alvarez led the way into the smaller sitting room, waited until they were seated, said: 'This will be a very sad time for you, Señora.' It was a presumption he made only because of convention. There was no touch of mourning in either her manner or her appearance.

'It was terrible to read about it. I couldn't believe it and made Larry find out for certain.'

'You have my sincere condolences, Señora.'

She brought a lace-edged handkerchief out of her handbag and dabbed the corner of each eye. 'So what happens now?'

'Funeral arrangements may be made after his body is released.'

She looked around the room and her gaze centred on the several silver figures on the mantelpiece above the large open fireplace. 'And what about the house?' She twisted an edge of the handkerchief between forefinger and thumb. 'I know it's no time since it happened, but I'm wondering if it's up to me to sort out everything.'

'Since there has not yet been time to find out to whom the Señor's estate now belongs, I fear I cannot answer you.'

'When will you know?'

'Perhaps there will be something here to tell me who are his law advisers; if so, I'll get in touch with them and they will know who are his beneficiaries.'

'This place is all his, isn't it?'

'As far as I am aware, Señora.'

She again looked around the room, mentally valuing what she saw.

'She was his wife,' Grant said roughly, 'so she's a right to what he's left.'

'That will be a question for the lawyers to answer. And perhaps I should point out that most of his capital may well have been kept outside Spain and Britain – that is a common habit of Britishers who live here.'

'And if that's what happened?'

'Then, as I understand it, provided he executed a valid will covering his assets in each country in question, those assets will not be touched by Spanish law – assuming, of course, no one is naive enough to bring their presence to the minds of the Spanish authorities.'

'What wills did Scott make?'

'I do not know.'

'Why not?'

'Larry,' she said, 'it's not what happens to his money that matters now, it's just trying to come to terms with his death.'

Yet only moments before, Alvarez thought sardonically, her interest had exclusively been in what would happen to the home and its contents.

Grant ignored her words. 'Have you looked for his wills? I'll bet not. That would be too much like work. Forget it – we'll do the searching.'

'I think not,' Alvarez said curtly.

'She's his wife, so she can do what she wants . . .'

'Since I am conducting an investigation, the señora may not do anything connected with the señor without my permission.'

'An investigation into what?'

'The cause of his death.'

'He drowned, didn't he?'

'We do not yet know why he drowned.'

'Even for this poxy little island, that's rich! When a bloke gulps water into his lungs, he drowns. Got it?'

'The question is, why did he fall into the swimming pool?'

'He tripped.'

'You can be certain that is what happened because you were here?'

'Of course I bleeding wasn't. Listen, mate, I've just about had enough of this . . .'

'Larry, please,' she pleaded, 'don't get so angry.'

'What d'you expect me to do when it's like talking to a moron? Why did he fall into the pool? Because he bloody well tripped, that's why.'

'Then why,' Alvarez asked quietly, 'didn't the señor just swim to the side and get out?'

'How am I supposed to know that?'

'It seemed you knew all the answers.'

Grant became sullenly silent.

'Señora,' Alvarez said, 'I need to ask you some questions.'

'But why?' she replied.

'Because I have to decide whether someone was responsible for Señor Muir's death.'

'You're . . . you're saying it wasn't an accident?'

'I do not yet know.'

'But why think—'

'Just shut it!' Grant said crudely.

She looked uneasily at him.

'You live where, Señora?' Alvarez asked.

'In England; near Dorking.'

'You have been separated from your husband for some time?'

'Yes.'

'Why did you separate?'

'It's none of your bleeding business,' Grant said angrily.

Alvarez spoke mildly. 'Everything is my business until I know whether or not it's important.'

'This ain't.'

'I will be the judge of that.'

Grant spoke to Jemima. 'We're getting the hell out of here.'

'You will not leave until I say you may,' Alvarez corrected.

'We don't need your permission—'

'You do; or would you rather I arrested you?'

Grant's expression remained aggressive, but, finally accepting Alvarez's authority, he did not argue any further.

'Señora, why did you separate from your husband?'

'It's him made me leave because I complained about him chasing after every woman he met. He said he'd give me a place to live. After I'd moved in, I discovered I was just a tenant and I couldn't afford the rent.'

'Did you see him often after the separation?'

'Tried to, but he'd sold the house. Didn't know where he was until the solicitor told me he was living here.'

'Why were you employing a solicitor?'

'To get some money out of him.'

'Did you succeed?'

'Did I hell! He'd cleared off. I went to a solicitor and told him to make the bastard pay up as I was his wife. I should have known Scott wasn't that soft. The solicitor told me he'd moved all his money out of the country and any action against him was not only difficult, an order to pay me something would likely be worthless. Which left me near skint.'

'So what brought you to this island?'

'I learned—'

Grant interrupted her. 'She learned he was living here.'

'The solicitor phoned me one day,' she said. 'I thought if I came here and talked to him and said—'

Grant again interrupted her. 'She reckoned she could persuade him to do the right thing and give her some money.'

'And did you ask him if he would do that, Señora?'

'Yes.'

'Was Señor Grant with you?'

'Course I was,' Grant said.

'You didn't think that inadvisable in the circumstances.'

'The circumstances was, she needed someone with her because she was scared.'

'Of what were you scared, Señora?'

'He could get real angry.'

'And you expected him to become angry?'

'I thought when I told him—'

Yet again, Grant cut short her words. 'She thought he'd likely get nasty when she told him it was his duty to give her some money, seeing as she was still his wife.'

'So how did he react to the request?'

'Said he'd think about it,' Grant replied.

'That was when?'

'Friday.'

'Thursday,' she corrected.

'And you returned here today for what reason exactly?'

'Ain't that obvious?' Grant said. 'To find if he was going to give her something.'

'But you knew he was dead.'

Grant swore.

She said, her voice high: 'Living in this house, rolling in money and me, his wife, near skint. He owed it.'

'How long were you living with your husband, Señora?'

'For nine years, with him jumping from my bed into any other he could find.'

'During those nine years, what was his state of health?'

For a moment, the question seemed to confuse her, then she said: 'There wasn't anything wrong with him, if that's what you mean. When a man humps morning, noon, and night, he's got to be fit to start with.'

'He was never in hospital?'

'Only after the car crash.'

'Was he seriously injured in that?'

'At first they said he wasn't, then he got put in intensive care and the specialist was telling me to be prepared.'

'Because he might die?'

'Or live,' she said with a bitterness she instantly regretted.

'If he hadn't been badly injured, why was he in intensive care and in danger of dying?'

'I don't know. Something to do with bleeding.'

'They couldn't stop his bleeding?'

'I can't remember.'

Or hoped he would believe she couldn't. Because she knew that any wound Muir suffered could become fatal . . .

'Can you tell me where you were between five Saturday afternoon and midday Sunday?'

'Why?' she asked uneasily.

'Because he's thick enough to think we did the bastard in,' Grant said.

'But . . . but we couldn't have done a thing like that.'

'Where were you?' Alvarez asked a second time.

'At the club.'

'What club and where was it?'

'I don't remember . . .'

'It'll save time and perhaps a lot of trouble if you try harder.'

'We was told about this club with great acts,' Grant said.

'They weren't great, they were just sick,' she muttered.

'So there's a lot of people like sick acts.'

'Especially when they're real tight.'

'All right, I had a skinful, but it was all good for a laugh.'

'The management didn't think so.'

'Stupid sods!'

'Where was this club?' Alvarez asked.

'I don't know one place from another.'

'What was its name?'

'Club Gusto.'

'The hottest show in town,' Grant said.

'Sick!' she said.

'Was it in Playa Los Arboles?'

'I think that's right. You know the club?' she asked.

'By reputation . . . When did you get there?'

'He was in such a hurry, we arrived before six and it didn't open until nine.'

'So what did you do for the three hours?'

'There wasn't anything to do except to go to the bar next door.'

'You were there until the club opened?'

'Yes.'

'When did you leave the show?'

'I wanted to come away—'

'And I didn't,' interrupted Grant, 'so we stayed until the place shut.'

'Which was when?'

'Could've been any time.'

'Just after four and he was too far gone to drive,' she said. 'So I had to drive and was worried because I'd never driven abroad before. And we got lost and looked like we were going to run out of petrol and it was a goddamn nightmare.'

'Where are you staying?' Alvarez asked.

'What's that matter?' Grant demanded.

'Hotel Cristina, down by the sea,' she said.

'Then I will contact you there if I need to speak to you again . . . You're free to leave now.'

Grant stood. She did the same, then said: 'If you find out about his will . . .'

'Should it concern you, I will let you know.'

'You've got to understand we just couldn't—'

'Come on,' Grant said roughly. 'If he likes to think we did the bastard in, let him.'

She followed Grant out into the hall. Alvarez heard the sounds of their feet on the marble floor, the creak of one of the halves of the front door being opened, the slam of its being shut. Had Grant had a hand in Muir's death, surely he would never have spoken so wildly? Yet perhaps he had done so because he was smart enough to make use of such an assumption. And it was interesting to remember how often he had interrupted what she'd been about to say – because he was afraid of where her words might lead?

Nine

Dolores said, her words sharp: 'Clearly, I have been wasting my time.'

Jaime looked across the dining table at Alvarez, who shrugged his shoulders; Isabel and Juan suffered the sense of uncertain guilt which their mother's annoyance always raised in their minds.

'Of course, it was stupid of me to take so much care. Would you not agree?' she asked Alvarez.

'I'm not certain . . .'

'My stupidity is that I spend hours in the kitchen, as hot as the fires of hell, because I believe a family should eat well—'

It seemed he was the target of her annoyance. 'Which they do. Magnificently well,' he added hurriedly.

'—should eat well. Yet what happens? When I serve espinagada, it is scorned.'

'Scorned? When it's even tastier than usual, which I'd have said was impossible.'

'Then why have you eaten so little?'

He looked down at his plate and saw the large portion of pastry filled with eel, garlic, parsley, peas, spinach, onions, and seasoning, still on it. 'I've been so slow eating not because I didn't like it – truly, it is very tasty – but I've been thinking.'

'About a woman, Uncle?' Juan asked.

'How dare you say such a thing,' Dolores snapped.

'You say that when Uncle acts dreamy, he's—'

'One more word and you spend the rest of the evening in your bedroom . . . There is some espinagado left, but I doubt anyone wants any more.'

Jaime, Isabel, and Juan assured her they would love some more, hoping to distance themselves from Alvarez. She served them, then herself. She ate a mouthful, sighed. 'When a man thinks of a woman, his hunger is not for food.'

'You said—' Juan began.

'That you will be silent.'

Juan's resentment increased as Isabel smiled mockingly at him.

'What's been bothering my mind,' Alvarez said between mouthfuls, 'is the case I'm working on.'

'Since when have you brought your work to the meal table?'

'It's a very difficult case.'

'As my mother used to say, "There is only one difficulty which prevents a man eating and drinking too much."'

'For your information, the only woman in this case is mutton dressed as lamb.'

'Mutton has more taste.' Jaime sniggered.

Dolores faced her husband. 'You speak from experience?'

'Of course not.'

'Perhaps you think of me as mutton?'

'For God's sake, all I meant . . . They do say . . .'

'I'm sure they say many things to which some husbands will eagerly listen. Enrique, there is very little left, but troubled as you are, I am certain you will not want it, so I—'

'On the contrary, I'd really like it.'

'You think you will have time between thoughts to enjoy it?'

'Ten times over.'

'Then pass your plate.'

While she placed the last of the espinagado on to his plate, he poured himself more wine. A moment ago, he'd been the target of her annoyance, now he seemed to be forgiven. To try to follow a woman's mind was to enter a labyrinth.

Fifteen minutes later, the children cleared the table and went out into the road to meet friends and play, while Dolores began to wash up in the kitchen. Jaime poured himself a large brandy, pushed the bottle across the table, said in a low voice: 'Is she really ancient?'

'Who?' Alvarez asked, his mind having been a long way away.

'This woman who's got you so excited, you're off your grub.'

'I have not—' He stopped. A straight denial would never convince Jaime, whose imagination was limited, but very active. 'She's far from good looking and is old enough to have a toy-boy in tow.' He poured himself another brandy.

'That's genuine?'

'Unfortunately.'

The note of regret convinced Jaime. 'So what's the problem?'

'I have to decide whether the señor died from accident, manslaughter, or murder.'

'What señor?'

'Señor Muir who owned Sa Rotaga.'

'What happened?'

'He drowned in his swimming pool. But how did he suffer the wounds which caused internal bleeding that made him so weak, he fell in and hadn't the strength to save himself? If he ran into, or fell on to, something, it was an accident; if someone deliberately hit him, it was murder or manslaughter. I can't find anything on which he could have been accidentally wounded, the laboratory people can't suggest what sort of weapon might have been used, so I now have to look for motive. Was it money? Was it sex?'

'There is another woman who isn't mutton?'

'I haven't met her yet, but from all accounts she's SEX in capital letters.'

'If I were rich—' Jaime began, speaking more loudly than he had intended.

There was a call from the kitchen. 'And what if you were rich?' Dolores asked.

'I . . . I'd take you around the world on a luxury cruise.'

'Then I should ask myself what you were trying to hide from me to be foolishly spending so much money!'

Jaime muttered: 'Doesn't matter what you do, they're always suspicious.' He looked at the bead curtain as he listened to the sounds coming from the kitchen and, satisfied Dolores was not about to come through, poured himself a third brandy. 'Who's this wonderfully sexy woman?'

'She was the señor's latest.'

'You think she could be really hot?'

'Too scalding for you or me.' Alvarez looked at his watch. 'I suppose there's just about time.'

'To do what?'

'Have a word with someone to confirm what I've been told.'

'You're going out now to do some work?'

71

'That's right.'

'I'd more easily believe you'd won the lottery . . . You're off to see this woman.'

'I'm hoping to have a word with a husband.'

'You mean, you're hoping you don't.'

Elena lived on the conical hill about and on which Llueso had initially been built and immediately above her house was a heavily restored, circular look-out tower which had once been manned to give warning of invading Moors. Alvarez opened the front door of her house, which directly abutted on to the narrow road, stepped into the front room, furnished for formal occasions and seldom used at other times, called out: 'Elena.'

A man, his expression glowering, came through the far doorway. 'What do you want?'

Lorenzo was massively built, though not tall, and a physical challenge from him was to be avoided at all costs. Alvarez hurriedly said: 'You're Elena's husband?'

'Never mind who I am, who the hell are you and why d'you come in here, shouting her name?'

'I'd like a word with you—'

'And you won't like what you'll hear! Thought I was out, didn't you?' He bunched his fists.

Elena hurried through the far doorway.

'D'you know him?' Lorenzo shouted.

'Of course I do.'

'He thought I wasn't here and you and him—'

'Don't be so stupid. He's Enrique, in the Cuerpo; been at Sa Rotaga, investigating the señor's death like I told you.'

Lorenzo slowly lowered his fists.

'He gets some odd ideas,' she said.

One of which obviously was that anyone who looked twice at his wife would have just enough time to regret his rashness before he lost all interest in everything. 'I'm sorry to come here this late, but I'd no choice because of all the work in hand.'

'There's something you want?' she asked.

'I need to ask your husband something.' He paused. Someone as suspicious as Lorenzo might well take offence at his questions. It would be best to shift responsibility. 'My superior chief insists I talk to Lorenzo even though I said this was totally unnecessary since there was absolutely no reason to doubt what you'd told me; on the contrary, I said, there was every reason to accept it without a single reservation.' He judged his words had confused Lorenzo, but that was an advantage since confusion weakened angry suspicion. 'You remember telling me you and Pablo left Sa Rotaga just after five, Saturday afternoon?'

She nodded.

'Pablo drove you back here, so you arrived about when?'

'Maybe a quarter to. He's a slow driver because of Águenda – she won't let him drive quickly.'

Alvarez turned to Lorenzo. 'Where were you when Elena returned?'

'What's it to you?'

'Don't be any more stupid,' she said. 'Tell him.'

'It was Saturday, wasn't it? I finish work early.'

'So were you here when Elena arrived in Pablo's car?' Alvarez asked for the second time.

'I bloody didn't like it!'

'Sweet Mary!' she said, in exasperated tones. She faced her husband. 'You really think Pablo was going to try anything with me when Águenda's waiting for him? If she thought he'd put a hand on me, she'd have a gypsy's revenge.'

It seemed that here were two marriages which were going to last; the one defended by the husband's fists, the other by the wife's scissors. 'Did Elena stay in the house all evening?'

'Yes,' Lorenzo muttered angrily.

'And all night?'

'What are you—?'

'Stop thinking stupidities,' Elena snapped. 'Just tell him, was I here all night with you?'

'Why is he asking?'

'Was I here with you?'

'Of course you bleeding well was,' he shouted, 'or I'd have been after Pablo—'

'One day your ridiculous jealousy will have me in an asylum!'

As crazy as Lorenzo's attitude must seem to an outsider, Alvarez judged Elena secretly welcomed it because she saw it as evidence of the overwhelming love he had for her.

On Friday morning, Alvarez parked in front of Sa Rotaga. He did not immediately get out of the car, but after switching off the engine, sat and stared at the house. Don Moldanado had had the power of position and it had been that which had enabled him to eye his peasants and decide which young woman would next amuse him; in the modern world, wealth had given Muir a power which corrupted women; circumstances changed, consequences didn't.

He finally left the car, crossed to the porch, opened the right-hand door and stepped into the hall, called out. After a moment, Elena appeared. 'You again!'

'There's something I should have asked you last night, but forgot to do so . . . You're not looking too fit. Not ill, I hope?'

'A woman has much more to bear than a man.'

And made such a song and dance about some things. 'Why not leave and return home?'

She didn't bother to answer; women were born to be martyrs. She led the way into the sitting room, sat. 'Well?'

'Pablo told me yesterday,' Alvarez said, when comfortably seated, 'that when the two of you left here on Saturday, you passed another car on the dirt track and you recognized who was driving it.'

She fidgeted with a button. 'I only looked quickly. I thought I recognized the driver.'

'Who did you think it was?'

'Señor Locke.'

'Was he a friend of the señor's?'

'He came to the parties; and he called the previous afternoon.'

'On the Friday?'

'Isn't that usually the day before Saturday?' she asked sharply.

'So he spoke to the señor then?'

'He did not, because the señor was out.'

'Did Señor Locke say why he wanted to speak to Señor Muir?'

'Of course he did not.'

'Did he seem concerned Señor Muir was out? In other words, did you think it was something important that brought him here?'

'How would I know that?'

'Not directly, of course, but you might have gained an impression from his attitude.'

After a moment, she said: 'He . . .' then became silent.

'Tell me.'

'He seemed very upset about something, but was polite to me. He wasn't like the señor, he's a true señor.'

That made sense to Alvarez. Muir was granted the rank of señor – once a mark of social class – through wealth, Locke through manners. 'Returning to Saturday, you left here a short time after five and met this car, probably driven by Señor Locke?'

75

She nodded.

'What kind of car was it?'

'I can't tell what any of them are. But it was an estate.'

'Do you remember the colour?'

'Dark green,' she answered immediately. 'Like a frock I bought, but can't wear because Lorenzo says it's not decent just because of the neckline. I said, walk through the village and you'll see ten times more than I'm showing, but all he could shout was that foreigners don't know what decency is. It's such a nice frock.'

Her relationship with Lorenzo seemed more complicated than Dolores's with Jaime – in the unlikely event of Jaime's insisting on anything, it was very unlikely Dolores would meekly agree. 'You're being very helpful . . . Now tell me what you can about Señor Muir.'

'What is there to tell? He was very rich, knew many women, and when something was not as he wanted, he blamed everyone but himself.'

'Did he have a great number of friends?'

'Are people friendly with a rich man because of him or his wealth?'

'You're suggesting not many liked him for himself?'

'That would have been difficult.'

'Can you give me the names of those who came here?'

'Of those who spoke to me and were friendly, I can name some; but there were others who looked at me as if I always blow my nose on my fingers. I do not know their names.'

No matter how many times she had heard them. 'I'd be grateful if you'd write down any you can remember . . . Recently – say in the past week – did the señor have an argument with anyone?'

'He was always shouting at me when he was in a bad mood.'

'I really meant a row with someone who visited the house, or maybe you heard him rowing with someone over the telephone.'

'There was the woman who said she was Señora Muir.'

'Tell me about her.'

'She came here with a man . . .'

'When was this?'

She thought. 'My hands were really dirty because I was cleaning some of the silver and I do that on Thursdays. The señor wanted it looking really bright because that made people notice it. Must have been a week ago yesterday.'

'Did it surprise you when she said she was Señora Muir?'

Elena had been more than surprised since the señor had never mentioned a wife. She'd wondered how he would behave and it had taken no time to find out. She'd heard the row in the sitting room – he was shouting, the man was shouting, and the señora shouted louder than either of them.

'A really angry argument?'

'I've not heard much angrier.'

'In what sort of mood was the señor when the other two left?'

'He was smiling,' she answered, clearly perplexed by this.

'And in what sort of a mood were they?'

'Like . . . Well, like nothing was right.'

'Did you see them again?'

She shook her head.

'On Saturday, the señor entertained a lady?'

'If you wish to call her that.'

'Pablo seems to think the visit may not have been such a success for the señor?'

'Pablo has a mind like . . . like most men's.'

'Tell me what happened.'

At first she spoke slowly, searching for the words which

77

would express what she wanted to say; then, as she continued, she became more fluent. From the beginning, the relationship had not been like the others. The señor, usually so confident, had for once seemed uncertain – as if worried that for once his charm and money might not ensure an easy seduction. On the Saturday, he'd called for a special meal – only a man like he would think a meal might challenge a woman's virtue. When he'd returned from the port with the puta, he'd been almost nervous. And she? . . . Putas of her class knew how to excite their clients by exhibiting a little hesitation, perhaps even token opposition. Of course, they never lost trade through prolonged hesitation, let alone opposition, but this one had . . . A woman could usually tell what another woman thought . . .

And was always certain she knew exactly what a man was thinking, Alvarez mentally added.

In the puta's manner there had been a hint of something odd and difficult to identify – even for another woman. Amusement, sarcasm, contempt? . . . Elena became silent.

'She didn't enjoy the special meal you'd cooked, did she?'

'Hardly ate anything. Never mind I'd made the butcher give me his finest meat, which was meant to go to a restaurant; or that I had used all my skill in preparing the dish, even though it was a French one . . . Had I been allowed to cook entrecote amb albercocs, not even a puta could have left half her meal.'

'And afterwards they went upstairs.'

'Who told you that?'

'Pedro.'

'His tongue knows no barriers.'

'But it wasn't a happy after-lunch bon-bon for the señor?'

'Pedro also told you that? The man has a sink of a mind.'

'Are you saying he's wrong and the señor probably did enjoy himself?'

'I'm saying there are some things decent people do not put into words.'

'But now that they have been, what would you reckon happened?'

'If the señor was satisfied, he had a strange way of showing that.'

'Tell me.'

When the señor had reappeared, he'd been in a nasty temper. He'd rudely ordered Pedro to drive the puta to the port.

'What happened after they left?'

'Nothing.'

'Something must have done . . .'

'I said, nothing.'

'I'm only asking what he did.'

'How should I know?'

'Then what did you do?'

'The clearing-up.'

'Did you see the señor again before you left the house with Pedro?'

'No.'

'But once you were in the car, the señor came out of the house and seemed to want something?'

'Pedro thought he did and called out.'

'How did he respond?'

'Shook his head.'

'So you left?'

'I was in a hurry to get home to prepare the meal for Lorenzo.'

'As far as you could judge, there was nothing wrong with the señor at that time?'

'Wouldn't he have spoken had there been any trouble?'

'Yes, of course . . . Is there a safe somewhere in the house?'

'There's one in the room he called his office.'

'Will you show me where it is?'

She led the way out of the sitting room, past the dining room, turned into a small corridor which ended in the square office. She opened the shutters of the single window. The office held none of the luxury of the rooms they had left. The furnishings were minimal and the furniture functional. There was a half-filled bookcase, a desk on which was a computer, a filing cabinet, and a large and ugly free-standing cupboard. She crossed to the door beyond the cupboard and opened this to reveal a large combination safe, set into the wall.

He studied the safe briefly, said: 'People often can't trust their memories where numbers are concerned, so they write them down. Have you come across a piece of paper with numbers on it hidden somewhere in this room?'

'No,' she snapped, her expression suddenly hard.

He smiled. 'If there were a million euros in this safe, the door was open, and the señor a thousand kilometres away, I know you'd go to the stake rather than touch a single note.'

'Then why do you ask such a question?'

'Because I'm going to have to see what's inside the safe and if I can't find out what the combination is, I'll have to call out an expert from Palma to open it.'

There was a silence.

'When you clean a room,' he said quietly, 'you will dust every square centimetre. Perhaps you have come across a piece of paper with numbers on it hidden somewhere and thought no more about it until this moment?'

She folded her arms across her ample bosom and stared through the window. Finally, she made up her mind. 'There are some numbers on one of the photographs.'

He crossed to the fireplace. On the back of the fourth

framed photograph, which featured Muir and a redhead, was a square of paper on which were eight numbers.

She watched him carry the photograph over to the safe and spoke as he prepared to manipulate the dials. 'Is that all you want?'

'For the moment, thanks.'

'I've work to do.' She left, closing the door behind her.

The safe contained several files, cheque books, bank statements, documents, a passport, and three bundles of five hundred euro notes, two considerably thicker than the third. He stared at the money. When he had stilled Elena's fears that he might suspect her, he had casually talked about a million euros – a guess said the total of these three bundles would fall short of that amount, but it would still be in the hundreds of thousands. Each bundle was secured by two elastic bands; each was identified by a square of paper on which was written either the initials DV or VY. He counted. Each of the two large bundles totalled 300,000 euros, the small one, 30,000. He had never before had so much cash in front of himself. He prided himself on his honesty, yet wasted no time in returning the notes into the safe because no man could know for certain if there was a point at which he might succumb to temptation.

He leafed through the files and realized it would take a long time and much mental effort to discover if any information they contained might be of significance to the case. He bundled them up to take with him, closed the safe door, moved the dials, and placed the photograph of the redhead back on the mantelpiece.

Ten

Alvarez yawned. Was there anything more tiring than reading through pages of facts and figures, of legal documents, of handwritten notes? . . . He yawned again, leaned over and brought bottle and glass out of the bottom right-hand desk drawer, poured himself a drink. Experts said alcohol befuddled rather than sharpened the brain; experts made a science of denying pleasure.

He leaned back in the chair, glass in hand. He had supposed Muir to be fairly wealthy; he had been very wealthy. Assets in different forms had been held in several countries, mostly under holding companies, and it would need a far sharper brain to understand all the intricate financial details. What was of particular interest – and was comprehensible – was the sale of a building in London for two and a quarter million pounds, due to be completed very shortly. Jemima had said that when her husband had moved abroad, he had owned no assets in Britain against which a court order could be made to ensure she received a settlement. This sale proved her to have been misinformed. Or was that what she wanted others to believe? . . . If Muir had no assets in Britain, no threat of hers could have any substance; a plea for compassion was bound to be futile. So how could she have believed that to turn up at Sa Rotaga with her companion could help her cause? . . . It had taken her the best part of two years to face her husband. Because until very recently, she had accepted the futility of doing so? Then had she – through her solicitor? – discovered not all her husband's assets had yet been moved abroad and that he still owned – but not for much longer – property in the UK worth two and a quarter million pounds? And had she been about to blurt this out as her reason for coming to the island when Grant – with a far sharper mind – had cut her short because had she admitted she had learned about the property, it might be obvious she had come to threaten she would resume divorce proceedings and demand a share of what was available. And since Muir was notoriously hot tempered, she had needed Grant to protect her . . .

There were four wills, each covering assets in a different country, bequeathing his estates to trustees who were to found and support a UK charity, named the Scott Muir Trust Fund, for the benefit of women in financial trouble after being deserted by their husbands. Few Victorians had managed to climb quite so high up the ladder of hypocrisy.

Elena had been surprised that on the Thursday after a bitter argument with Jemima and Grant, Muir had been in a good temper. Was this because it had amused him to be able to tell Jemima that her threats were impotent because the sale would be completed before any action of hers could have effect?

He thought about the cash. 630,000 euros was a large sum of money – he had laboriously to convert it into pesetas before he could be certain quite how relatively large. On the 12th April, a similar sum in cash had been withdrawn from a bank in Liechtenstein. Why had Muir twice needed so much money? . . .

Amongst the files and bank statements had been a tourist guide for north Mallorca. Wondering why this should be in the safe, he had riffled through it and on page 46, above a coloured photograph of La Salinas, the nature reserve, had been written in pencil the figures 971 4634567. If the guide had not been left in the safe by mistake, then its presence had in some way to be significant, in which case, the handwritten phone number might also be significant . . .

He phoned Telefonica in Palma and asked the woman to whom he spoke to identify the holder of the number; she bad-temperedly agreed to do so. He went to drink, found the glass was empty. He put it down on the desk and studied it. He had promised himself to reduce his drinking and smoking for health reasons and he was a man of his word. But wasn't it mistaken masochism to deprive himself of pleasure now in the hope of future health when that was largely a matter of genes and luck, neither of which a drink could alter? He poured himself another brandy, slightly smaller, and lit a cigarette, assuring himself he would stub this out when half smoked. Moderation in all things was the sensible man's road to take . . .

He resentfully accepted the case was raising more questions than he was answering. Which meant he was being called upon to work even harder at a time of year when every sensible animal sought the shade and did nothing. If only he had found something with two thin, curved spikes in the grounds or pool complex at Sa Rotaga on to which Muir had clearly accidentally fallen. Then, there would have been no need to wonder if Jemima and Grant had spent all evening at a bar and Club Gusto as they claimed; that Pablo and Elena had probably passed Locke in his car on Saturday would have been of no account; the guide with the telephone number written in it could have been dismissed; and the money? . . . Rich men led rich lives.

He drained the glass, stubbed out the cigarette before it burned him, leaned back in the chair and closed his eyes the better to consider the problems which had to be addressed . . .

The phone awoke him.

'The number you wanted traced is in the name of Diego Vives and the address is seven, Carrer Tiziano, Cala Roig.' The woman's tone became school-marmish. 'It would help if the next time you want a tracing carried out, you give us at least some warning.'

And how did one give warning of something's being wanted before one knew it was? he silently asked as he replaced the receiver. He studied the name and address he'd written down on the back of an unopened envelope and wondered why they seemed to hold some significance when he knew no Diego Vives who lived in Cala Roig? On the point of accepting there was no significance, he remembered the initials on the smallest of the bundles of euro notes – DV. Coincidence? It wouldn't take much effort to find out, but it was a task best left until tomorrow . . . Except that tomorrow was Saturday. Still, it was a job that could be completed before midday and the start of his off-duty weekend.

Not so many years previously, Cala Roig had been just a W-shaped inlet in the rocky north coast which offered some shelter for the few fishermen who risked their lives in waters which could turn dangerous in a very short time and often held a current that could sweep a man to his death, however strong a swimmer – not that many of the fishermen could swim, preferring to place their trust in the saints. Then the tourists had arrived. Hotels were built on the eastern side of the wider inlet and they were followed by shops to serve the tourists; houses were needed by the people who worked in the hotels and shops; foreign residents wanted to live there and three separate urbanizacíons were developed. Yet despite all the hotels, shops, and houses, the pine trees, the stark, rocky mountains, and the water kept clear by the current combined to provide great beauty and this despite the final insult of a fourth urbanizacíon of cheap and tacky holiday homes on the slope of one of the enclosing mountains.

7, Carrer Tiziano was a small bungalow with many roof levels and little or no charm. Alvarez walked through the garden – in his opinion very sensibly growing only bushes and cacti which needed no attention – and tried the front door; it was locked. He knocked. The door was opened by a woman whose dark brown eyes, long, black hair, and sharp features suggested some Moorish ancestry. 'Señora Vives?' he asked.

'Yes?'

'I'm Inspector Alvarez of the Cuerpo General—' He was interrupted by the screams of an infant.

Uncertain what to do, uneasy to learn he was a detective, she hesitated.

'Calm the baby down and then we can talk,' he said. There were some who compared the cries of a baby to the singing of an angel; he did not.

She left the door open, hurried along a passage. He stepped into the very small hall and shut the door behind himself. When she returned, she held a baby in her arms. 'He's quiet like this.'

Since it was usually advantageous to gain the friendly approval of the person one was about to question, he said the baby looked a picture; he was not an art lover. 'I should like to speak to your husband.'

'What . . . Is something wrong?'

'Nothing to cause any worry. I just want to find out if he knows why your telephone number was written down in a guide book.'

'I don't understand.'

He smiled. 'Neither do I, which is why I'm hoping he'll be able to explain. Is he here?'

'He's gone to see his aunt, Doña Inés Terrasa.'

'Do you expect him back soon?'

'He'll be with her for lunch. She's old and lonely and likes to have someone to talk to.'

'Where does she live?'

'Near the glassworks.'

'The ones this side of Inca?'

She nodded.

Too far to be reached in a time that was reasonable on a Saturday morning.

The baby began to mewl and she murmured as she rocked him in her arms.

'I needn't bother you any longer. Will you just tell your husband I'll return before long to have a word.'

It was clear that Dolores was in a good mood. She made no comment before the meal when Jaime, believing her to be busy in the kitchen, was refilling his glass as she entered the room, and she had cooked cocarrois de peiox for supper.

'Only a genius could make a fish pasty taste as if it were filled with caviare,' Alvarez said, as he finished his last mouthful.

'And when have you ever tasted caviare?' she asked.

'Perhaps I never have, but I have read many times it is more delicious than ambrosia.'

'The more flowery a man's words, the sharper the hidden thorns.' But it was clear the words pleased her.

Jaime decided he could risk refilling his glass and emptied the bottle of Sangre de Torros into it, wondering, as he did so, why Alvarez could talk nonsense and escape Dolores's disapproval, whereas if he'd mentioned ambrosia, she would have snapped that his words were fuelled with alcohol.

Alvarez picked up the bottle, discovered it was empty, put it down again. 'I heard a name earlier which seemed to ring a bell, but I can't think why.' His words were edged with the annoyance provoked by the empty bottle.

Juan sniggered.

'What is your problem?' Dolores asked.

'Uncle knows so many ladies, he can't remember which one—'

'Stupidity has a senseless tongue.'

'But you do often say he—'

'Another word and there will be trouble.'

Juan scowled, Isabel grinned.

'There is another bottle of wine in the cupboard,' Dolores said.

The two men looked at each other, wondering whether her words concealed a trap.

'You don't want any more?'

Jaime finally leaned over and brought a bottle out of the sideboard. As he opened it, Dolores went through to the kitchen, to return with the sweet, Ous de neu. She accepted the words of surprised pleasure with little modesty. As she sat, having served everyone, she said: 'Enrique, what was the name to which you cannot put a face?' She glanced briefly at her son, who hastily concentrated on his food.

'Doña Inés Terrasa. I know I've come across it before, but I can't remember where or when.'

'She is the widow of Don Terrasa.'

He refrained from explaining he had realized that. 'And who was he?'

'A very great man when I was young; to us, he came

from a different world. How things have changed! Now, we do not bow our heads when the likes of him pass.'

It was doubtful if she had ever honestly bowed her head to anyone. 'Did he own an estate?'

'It stretched around the bay between the port and Playa Neuva and almost to Mestara. Of course, almost all has gone. He lived life as the rich did before democracy brought such taxes. And he was a noble gambler. When I think about it, I suppose his widow is relatively poor.'

'That'll be why the Wilderness is up for sale,' Jaime said.

'Impossible! She and her husband loved that land as they would have the son they were never able to have. In any case, it is a nature reserve.'

'It isn't.'

'Must you always speak from folly?'

'If it's protected, how come they built those holiday camps on it?'

For once, she could not think of an answer.

'Who said it was for sale?' Alvarez asked.

'I don't remember,' Jaime answered carelessly.

'If you spent less time in bars, you might still have a memory,' she snapped.

Her mood had clearly changed and the remainder of the meal was eaten in near silence. Jaime did not refill his glass.

Eleven

Alvarez awoke and, after the initial fear he must soon get up and work, remembered it was Saturday. He relaxed and his mind wandered freely until he recalled Jaime's lunch-time assertion that the Wilderness – the local name for some of the land between Port Llueso and Playa Neuva – was for sale. It was an area he loved; a land of garriga – wild bushes, herbs, brambles, grasses – and a favoured resting place for migratory birds; the home of several species of small reptiles; some of the island's rarer flowers and orchids grew there. A man could walk it and, provided he did not look too far east or west, believe himself far away from civilization . . . A few years previously, it had been larger but, as always, money had proved its poisonous quality. A few hectares, some of which bordered the bay, had been owned by a man from Palma whose passion for gambling had been far greater than his skill or luck. When his losses had become very considerable, he had sold the land and it had been bought for a large sum by a property developer. People had laughed at such stupidity – permission to build would never be given. A holiday complex – ugly barrack-like buildings, tennis courts, bars, restaurants, parking area, lawns, lighting – proved them wrong. Yet there still remained enough land for the name, the Wilderness, not to be a mockery. Now it seemed there might be the threat of more development and the solitude, birds, reptiles, flowers, and orchids, the wild bushes and herbs, sprawling grasses, trails of brambles, would be further displaced, perhaps eradicated. Migratory birds would fly on, many to die from exhaustion . . . Was there no one willing to put beauty before profit?

As he dressed, it occurred to him to wonder if there could be a connexion between a possible sale of the Wilderness, the telephone number in the guide book, and the nephew of Doña Inés?

Alvarez could not remember when he had last voluntarily worked on a Saturday afternoon, but to save the past, he was prepared to forgo the pleasures of the present.

Son Formiou was a large possessío whose thick walls and small windows dated from a time when the fear of Barbary invaders had lessened, but there was still need to consider defence. The crumbling stonework, missing guttering, broken shutters, weed-filled courtyard, and tumbledown outhouses pointed to years of lack of maintenance and repair.

He climbed nine narrow stone steps to the wooden door, some three metres above ground level, and banged the knocker. To his left were brackets, set in the stone, which he identified as having once borne the weight of the heavy metal door pierced with small holes which had guarded the entrance – because of the narrowness of the steps, only one man at a time could climb them and as he ascended, he could be shot through one of the holes.

The door was opened by a man in his middle twenties who, because of beady brown eyes, a long nose, thin lips, and prominent teeth, Alvarez silently nicknamed 'Rat-face'. His general appearance aroused further dislike – long hair tied into a pony tail, an earring in one ear, a

T-shirt on which was printed in English 'Touchy-feely much appealy', frayed jeans, and colourful trainers.

'What d'you want?'

'A word with Doña Inés.'

'You can't.'

'Why's that?'

'Because I say.'

'Are you Diego Vives?'

'Piss off.'

'Inspector Alvarez, Cuerpo General de Policia.'

'You called at my place this morning?'

'That's right.'

Vives's tone became servile. 'I'm so sorry, Inspector. I should have realized. Do please come in.'

The hall was large, high, beamed, tiled with red-veined marble, and hardly furnished; four leather-backed and string-strung chairs were set against one of the walls; in front of the very wide fireplace was a table with overhanging and faded woollen blanket under which was an unpolished braser – a brass charcoal brazier; in the centre, held in an elaborately worked wrought-iron container, was a flower pot in which grew a sickly aspidistra; on the far wall hung a heavily framed oil painting so darkened by dust and age that it was impossible at any distance to make out its subject.

'I'm sorry to have mistaken you for a casual caller, Inspector; very sorry. I should have realized you were someone important.'

Vives's manner had become mockingly servile. Years before, Alvarez reflected with nostalgia, he would have been simply servile. 'Now we've established identities, I'd like a word with Doña Inés.'

Vives was about to reply when a middle-aged woman, face heavily lined by past endless hours working in blazing sun or biting wind, came into the hall through a doorway with arched heading. 'She's calling for you.' Her rough accent identified her as coming from Mestara; it was claimed that such inhabitants chewed and swallowed half their words.

'Tell her I'll be with her as soon as possible, but we have a visitor.'

She returned the way she had come.

'My aunt is not well.' Vives tapped his head.

'I'm sorry to hear that.'

'So it is hopeless trying to talk to her. Today it is one of her really bad days and even Juana, who's worked here since before my uncle died, can't understand her much of the time.'

'Then I'll come back another day.'

'I can't guarantee she'll be any better.'

'Of course not.' Any and every guarantee he offered would be worthless. 'Since I can't talk to her, I can ask you a few questions.'

'How can I possibly help you?'

'That's what I'll find out. Shall we find somewhere to sit?'

Vives hesitated, seemed about to speak but didn't, led the way through the arched doorway into a room whose beamed ceiling was five metres high at the rise; the rock walls had once been coated with yeso to keep them smoothly white, but for many years this had not been done and in places the compacted yeso had flaked away; the six easy chairs had worn and stained velvet covering and the carpet, of traditional design, had threadbare patches; many of the floor tiles were chipped; there were no curtains over the two windows; the overhead light, with eight brackets, lacked three bulbs. It was a picture of decayed privilege.

Alvarez sat – the chair proved to be more solid than appearance had suggested. 'You knew Señor Muir.'

'Who?'

He repeated the name.

'Never heard of him.'

'He was an Englishman, as the name suggests.'

Vives crossed and uncrossed his legs, he looked quickly at Alvarez, met the other's gaze, hurriedly looked away.

'You did not know him?'

'I've just said.'

'Then I wonder why your home telephone number should be written down in a tourist guide which belonged to him?'

'That's impossible.'

'It's fact. When did you learn he was dead?'

'Can't you understand I've never heard of him before now?'

There was a silence.

'Can you suggest an answer?' Alvarez asked.

'To what?'

'To how your telephone number came to be written down in his guide?'

'It can't have been his.'

'It was in his safe.'

'Then he wrote down a wrong number.'

'Most unlikely.'

'Then maybe . . . Was he kind of middle aged, taller than you, dressed real smart, and talking terrible Spanish?'

'I suppose one might say that begins to describe him.'

'He must have been the one I helped!'

'When?'

'I don't know exactly. Maybe six weeks ago.'

'Helped how?'

'It was like this. I was driving to the port and came up to a car with a puncture; a big car, a Jaguar. The driver was standing and looking like he didn't know what to do, so I stopped. He said his back was bad and it hurt too much to

94

undo the wheel nuts and when he'd tried to use his mobile to call his garage, the battery was flat.'

'You understood all this even though his Spanish was so poor?'

'I speak enough English and when he knew that, he spoke English.'

'What did you do? Call the garage on your mobile?'

'Changed the wheel for him.'

'Very noble minded. But how does that explain the number in the guide?'

'When I'd finished, he offered me ten euros. I wouldn't take it, said I'd helped him like I'd help anyone. So he thanked me a second time – the English are polite, aren't they?'

'When they're sober.'

'He got into his car and started the engine, then lowered the window and shouted he'd like to have a word with me another day and what was my name and telephone number. So I told him. He must have written the number down.'

'But not your name.'

'Easier to remember.'

'Did he get in touch with you again?'

'No.'

'I'd say that's a load of balls.'

'Straight, it's what happened. I swear it is.'

Alvarez was less certain than his words had suggested. Just occasionally, an apparent absurdity turned out to be true and if one failed to acknowledge that possibility, one could land very heavily in the mire . . . 'Your aunt is mentally disturbed?'

'Mentally kaput much of the time; doesn't understand anything. The doctor says it's old age.'

'Who looks after her?'

'Juana. Can be as sour as an unripe cacki, but she's devoted to my aunt.'

'So does she look after your aunt's business affairs?'

'No. She can read, but only slowly, and she's hopeless with figures.'

'Then who does?'

'I do. But my uncle was a gambler and when he died, there was only this place and a bit of land left, so there's not much needs doing.'

'Do you have power of attorney?'

'I don't see how that concerns you.'

'Nor do I until I know the answer.'

After a pause, Vives said: 'When she first started going downhill, she asked me to cope with things because she could trust me; the doctor said she was still sufficiently sound in mind to give me power of attorney, so that's what happened.'

'Then you've control of everything she owns and she's unlikely ever to challenge anything you do?'

'She knows I wouldn't do anything that could possibly upset her.'

'How can she be so certain if her brain's gone?'

'I've always honoured the trust she put in me.'

'It's good to hear . . . Returning to Señor Muir. There's something else which puzzles me. You met him only the once when you changed the wheel for him, so why would he have maybe already given you thirty thousand euros and reckon to do the same again soon?'

'What are you on about?' Vives asked hoarsely.

'In the safe, along with the tourist guide, were bundles of notes and on one of them was a piece of paper with your initials on it.'

'That's ridiculous.'

'DV aren't your initials?'

'They're someone else's.'

'You don't think he'd intended that money as a gift to you for your kindness?'

'You think someone's going to hand over thirty thousand just for changing a wheel?'

'It seems unlikely, but the English do strange things.'

'That would be bloody ridiculous.'

'But very welcome?'

'Of course it would be.'

'You wouldn't call yourself well off?'

'Me? If you saw my house—'

'I did, when I spoke to your wife.'

'Like a rabbit hutch. And now there's the kid. Do you know what it's like trying to sleep when a kid's screaming its head off?'

'Thankfully, no . . . So you don't think Señor Muir intended to give you this money had he lived?'

'I'm bloody certain he didn't.'

'You've not done any work for him which would justify such a reward?'

'What are you suggesting now?'

'Just trying to tie up loose ends and finishing with a granny knot . . . For the record, answer my last question.'

'I've not seen or heard from him since I changed the wheel.'

'Then that leaves me trying to find someone with the same initials . . . Thanks for your help.'

Alvarez was glad to leave a house which had known prosperity, but now only decay. As he drove along the coastal road between Playa Neuva and Port Llueso – the bay to his right was more beautiful than ever in the bright sunshine – he accepted he'd wasted a Saturday afternoon. He'd learned nothing which either confirmed or denied that the money in the safe was in some way connected with a sale of the Wilderness.

Twelve

On Monday, as always, Alvarez arrived at his office expecting the worst – mail which needed an immediate response, telephone calls which demanded immediate action . . . There was no mail and no phone calls. He could hardly have been more cheerful when he left the post and made his way to Club Llueso for his merienda.

As he approached the bar, he said: 'One cortado and—'

'One coñac,' interrupted the bartender. 'And since a change is said to be as good as a rest, how about a small coñac?'

'Make it a large change with a larger coñac.'

'Plus ça change, plus c'est la même chose, as a drunken Frenchman said when he insisted on telling me about his four divorces and five marriages.'

'Obviously, a glutton for punishment.'

'By now, he's probably choked.' The barman filled a container with ground coffee, clipped it into the espresso machine. He picked up a bottle of Soberano and poured a brandy. 'Is something wrong?'

'Why d'you ask?'

'You sound almost cheerful.'

'It's Monday morning and there's not been a word from my superior. I think he must have unexpectedly gone on holiday.'

At twelve fifteen, he had bitter reason to remember his words.

'What the devil do you think you're doing?' was Salas's greeting over the telephone.

'With reference to what, Señor?'

'You've caused so much trouble, you don't know to which particular act of idiocy I'm referring?'

'As far as I know—'

'A discussion that must prove short and without point . . . I have had the minister complaining in very strong terms about the conduct of a member of the Cuerpo. At first, his anger was such I couldn't understand to whom he was referring, but when he spoke of incompetent stupidity, I realized you must be concerned. I hastened to explain you had joined the Cuerpo before the standards of entry had been raised – indeed, one could say that there were no standards – but this failed to pacify him and he insisted that since I was in command, I must bear full responsibility for the actions of someone who took leave of his senses. Where is the justice in that?'

'Señor, I fear I don't understand what is the problem . . .'

'Of course not since to you, the most extraordinary behaviour appears to be normal.'

'What possible reason could any minister have to make a complaint about me?'

'You don't think that destroying an innocent person's privacy on spurious grounds and browbeating her nephew on no grounds at all, might constitute good reason to those who believe in democracy?'

'Then . . . it sounds as if the complaint maybe came through Diego Vives?'

'On behalf of his aunt, Doña Inés Terrasa, who, I am informed, judged by the standards of this island, should be considered as being almost of high birth and standing.'

'All I did was ask Vives a few questions.'

'A question can be asked politely and tactfully, or with

rude incompetence. There is no need to enquire in which mode these questions were asked.'

'Señor, why should a minister concern himself with the matter?'

'That is not a question for you to ask.'

'But it must make one wonder if the minister is a friend or even a relation of Doña Terrasa.'

'Are you so lacking in sensibility that you now see fit to make a despicable inference?'

'It was so small a matter that normally no minister would think of concerning himself with it. And even if he did, would, because of his office, most certainly not interfere.'

'You regard yourself as an authority on a minister's position and duties?'

'Which minister is complaining?'

'That is no concern of yours.'

'I just wonder . . . It occurs to me that perhaps he is the Minister for Sustainable Development?'

There was no answer.

'Because if so, he's the final arbiter with respect to certain applications for property development, isn't he?'

'My God, what are you now suggesting?'

'That perhaps I underrated the nephew. I questioned him—'

'Why?'

'To discover whether he could help me establish the truth about Señor Muir's death.'

'Why should you believe that possible?'

'In the señor's safe was a tourist guide and on the top of the page describing the Wilderness – that is an area of untouched land between Port Llueso and—'

'There is no call for an uninformed lecture on the physical features of this island.'

'I think they may be important in this instance, Señor. Written on top of that page in the guide was the telephone number of Vives's home.'

'Of no significance.'

'Why should Señor Muir make a note of Vives's telephone number?'

'Neither of us can ever know.'

'I think it's possible to guess. Also in the safe were many papers and a large number of five hundred euro notes, totalling six hundred and thirty thousand euros. That's one hundred and four million, five hundred and eighty thousand pesetas, forgetting the euro cents which are hardly important . . .'

'As unimportant as everything else you have been saying.'

'One bundle of notes of thirty thousand euros bore the initials DV. Diego Vives. Bank statements show that a similar total sum was withdrawn early in the year from a Swiss bank . . . No, that's wrong. It was a Liechtenstein one . . .'

'Goddamn it, Alvarez, I've far too much work to do to listen to meaningless verbal rambling.'

'Señor, would you hold it so meaningless if I add it is rumoured the Wilderness is for sale?'

'What are you talking about? What is the Wilderness?'

'I did try to explain earlier, but you told me you were uninterested in the physical features of this island.'

'When speaking to you, it becomes difficult to be interested in anything.'

'The Wilderness is the last remaining, largely unspoilt land surrounding Llueso Bay and Doña Terrasa owns it. If sold with permission to develop were given, the value of the land would be immense; the profit to be made from the development as great, or greater.'

There was a long silence. Salas broke it. 'Are you now daring to suggest . . . I refuse to put it into words.'

'Then I don't think I can answer you, Señor.'

There was another long silence.

'Did you ask Vives to explain how his telephone number came to be in the guide in Señor Muir's safe?'

'That is why I went to Doña Terrasa's house after I spoke to Vives's wife and she told me her husband was at Son Formiou. It appears Doña Terrasa's mind is too clouded for her to understand much and certainly not—'

'What was his explanation?'

'One day he was driving along the bay road and came across a car which had suffered a puncture; the owner, Señor Muir, was unable to change the wheel due to a bad back. He changed it for Señor Muir, who offered money which he refused; when he was about to drive away, he was asked for his telephone number.'

'Then there is a simple explanation as to why the number was written down.'

'Strange things do happen, true, but looking at all the facts, remembering the thirty thousand euros, considering Vives's character and the power of attorney he has on his aunt's property—'

'Have you proved Señor Muir did not suffer a puncture and Vives did not change the wheel?'

'It's very difficult, often impossible, to prove a negative . . .'

'Which is one reason why you will not pursue this absurd, infamous, libellous nonsense any further.'

'Don't you think—'

'If you wish to continue in your job until you retire with a pension, you will obey my orders. Is that crystal clear?'

'Yes, Señor.'

Alvarez slowly replaced the receiver. He had been

speaking to a worried man – a superior chief was no match for a minister, even if only a minister in the regional autonomous government. Yet how much less of a match was a humble inspector?

Alvarez braked his Ibiza to a halt in front of four steps leading up to the small porch, on the walls of which were potted geraniums that provided splashes of colour. Even thirty years before, few flowers had been grown because one did not waste energy and time on something that provided no return – beauty had never lessened hunger. But the foreigners had introduced cultivated gardens, garden centres had become established to provide the plants and machines these wanted, and eventually the Mallorquins had also started to grow daffodils, petunias, pansies, cannas, agapanthus, passion flowers . . .

He climbed the steps, pressed the bell, turned and looked at the small caseta, less than a hundred metres away and within the grounds. Before this house had been built, the owners of the property had lived in that caseta. It had provided no comfort, only primitive shelter; the new house was almost certain to be filled with comfort. Sixty years ago, the ordinary Mallorquin could, perhaps with a little help, afford to buy the caseta; today, even with considerable help, he was very unlikely to be able to afford a house such as Ca Na Aila. As circumstances changed, there were winners and there were losers, but most remained losers.

The door was opened by a woman, dressed in a flowing cotton robe over a swimming costume, who approached late middle age with grace; when young, he judged her to have been very attractive. 'Señora Locke?'

'Yes,' Laura answered in Spanish.

He introduced himself in English. 'I apologize for

bothering you at this time of the evening, Señora, but there is something I should like to ask your husband.'

She frowned slightly. 'Is it . . . ? Come on in.' She held the panelled door, the wood in many dark brown shades, fully open. 'We're out by the pool,' she added, as he stepped inside.

The furnishings and furniture of the room they went through spoke of taste and an income to meet that taste. Locke sat at a table under the covered patio.

'Inspector Alvarez wants a word with you, Keir.'

Locke came to his feet. 'How d'you do.'

Alvarez had learned that this greeting was not the excuse for a medical summary of his health. 'Good evening, Señor. As I said to your wife, I am sorry to bother you, but I do need to ask you some questions.'

'No bother. Presumably, something has cropped up?'

'That is so.'

'Then before you tell us what the problem is, we've been having drinks, so let me offer you one. What would you like?'

'May I have a coñac with just ice?'

As Locke left to go indoors, Laura said, 'Do sit, Inspector.'

They both sat. He looked across the pool at the lantana hedge in flower, then at the mountains which enclosed Festna Valley and was yet again perplexed by the fact that the mountain to the right was covered with pine trees, the one to the left, separated by no more than four hundred metres, was bare rock; why the difference? . . . He realized he'd been silent for quite some time. 'You have a very nice home, Señora.'

'We were lucky that the house was on the market when we came here; we liked it so much more than others which were for sale.'

Even more lucky to be able to afford it! Now it must be worth many, many euros.

'Do you live here, Inspector?'

'In the village.'

'Then you may be able to tell me something. We have friends who are coming here and they asked when the Moors and Christians took place – they're very keen on the traditions. Is it, as someone said, at the beginning of next month?'

'On the second.'

'Would you describe it as being held mainly for the locals or the tourists?'

'Wholly for the islanders. But, of course, many tourists like to watch.'

'Sam will be glad to hear that. He's always saying that a flood of tourists must turn traditions into tourist shows, so that they lose their meanings.'

'We islanders are conservative by nature and so we want to keep our past true.' He might have added that there were times when to want to do something did not mean it would be done. There were fiestas in other parts of the island which had forgotten the past and played to the present.

'It's great to hear you say that.' She smiled.

She was someone whose warmth of character became very quickly apparent and he found himself, perhaps absurdly, feeling glad that his remarks had pleased her.

Locke returned, handed Alvarez a glass in which three cubes of ice floated in a large brandy, sat. 'Do help yourself to olives.' He indicated an earthenware dish in which were olives stuffed with anchovies. He raised his glass. 'Good health.'

Alvarez responded to the greeting, drank. It was brandy of a better quality than he normally enjoyed; riches might be unable to buy happiness, but they could provide a very good substitute. He helped himself to an olive.

'You've something to ask me?' Locke said.

'Yes, Señor. I'm investigating the unfortunate death of Señor Muir.' His answer plainly disturbed them.

'That suggests it wasn't the straightforward accident we've all believed?'

'We think not.'

'In what way?' Laura asked sharply.

'Laura, don't you think—' Locke began.

She interrupted him. 'Didn't Scott drown?'

'Death was due to drowning, Señora, but it is the cause of his falling into the swimming pool which concerns me.'

'Why?'

'We really shouldn't—' Locke began.

She interrupted her husband a second time. 'Why?' she repeated.

'Before his death, Señor Muir suffered two small wounds in his side.'

She stared at her husband, her expression shocked.

'The stab wounds were not deep and normally would not have proved fatal, but the señor suffered from an unusual complaint which meant that his blood did not clot and he became very weak and disorientated from the internal loss of blood. We surmise he was by his swimming pool, lost his balance, fell in and did not have the strength, perhaps even the will, to save himself.'

'You're saying someone deliberately killed him?'

'Death may not have been intended.'

'No,' she said shrilly.

Locke spoke hurriedly. 'My wife is easily shocked. To meet someone at his party and then learn he has died is bad enough, but to think he had been deliberately wounded is worse.'

'It is very understandable the señora should be upset—'

She interrupted him. 'Why have you come here?'

'I understand you and your husband were friends of Señor Muir.'

'We weren't.'

'What Laura means,' Locke said, 'is that the relationship is best described by saying we were acquaintances rather than friends.'

'Then you did not visit him very often?'

'Only when we had to,' she answered.

'"Had to", Señora?'

'A typical example of English verbal complications,' Locke said. 'We certainly weren't ever obliged to meet him; we did so when for one reason or another, it seemed reasonable to do so.'

'As on the Friday before his death?'

'He didn't—' Laura began, then stopped.

'Is that when I went along to his place?' Locke said, speaking as casually as possible.

'Elena told me it was when you called,' Alvarez said.

'Then it's probably right. I'm afraid I find one day merges into another and I can never place a particular one.'

'I understand he was out?'

'That's so.'

'Why did you call there, Señor?'

'Obviously, to speak to him.'

'About what?'

'It was a private matter.'

'I should like to know what it concerned.'

'I'm sorry, I don't see I'm obliged to tell you. Especially as there was no meeting.'

'Did you return at another time to speak to him?'

'No.'

'Then it was not important?'

'Why are you asking us all these questions?' Laura demanded angrily.

'I have to discover who inflicted the wounds Señor Muir suffered.'

'You think we can begin to help you?'

Locke said: 'The inspector obviously has to have a word with anyone who knew Scott.'

'We can't help.'

She failed to realize that the sharp emotion with which she spoke must raise a question mark in a listener's mind; her husband did.

'We may think we can't possibly know anything, dear, but we could be wrong. Something that seems to us of no account whatsoever, might interest the inspector.' Locke turned to Alvarez. 'I'm afraid Laura's more disturbed by the news than I thought. This sort of thing does often emotionally affect a woman very considerably.'

'Indeed.' But what exactly was it that was so affecting her?

'If there is some way in which we can help, perhaps we could do so as quickly as possible?'

'Of course . . . The medical evidence is no more certain than that Señor Muir died during the Saturday night and this makes it very difficult to judge when he received the wounds. What is certain is that just after five o'clock, Elena and Pablo – the maid and the gardener – saw him and since he indicated nothing was wrong, we know he was injured after that time. This means we have to learn who visited his house after five o'clock.' He lifted up his glass and drank slowly; her frightened concern became ever more evident. 'As Elena and Pablo drove away from Sa Rotaga, they passed a car going in the opposite direction. She thought she knew who the driver was.'

108

'Who?' Laura finally asked, her voice strained.

'Your husband, Señora.'

'No!'

'She accepts her identification was not exactly a very strong one . . .'

'An impossible one.'

'Laura,' Locke began.

'That's when we were with Evelyn and Neville.'

'Don't you think—'

'We took them a sponge cake and stayed at their place until after supper. Surely you remember?' She faced Alvarez again. 'The maid has to be totally mistaken. Maybe it was someone who vaguely resembled Keir, but it wasn't he. It's so easy to be wrong when one sees someone for only a moment, especially when the sharp sunshine creates deep shadows.'

'That is very true. However, Señora, I'm sure you'll understand that as a matter of routine, I will have to ask your friends to corroborate what you have just said, so will you be kind enough to tell me what their surname is and where they live?'

'Evelyn and Neville Marsh. Their house is Ca'n Bastoync, in El Montaje . . . Since we were there, my husband can't possibly have been anywhere near Scott's house.'

'Of course not.'

'Then that's sorted out?'

'And I can leave you in peace, Señora, after apologizing for any trouble I have caused.' Alvarez stood; Locke did the same. 'Señor, I remember there is just one more question I have to ask. What kind of car do you own?'

Locke hesitated, then said: 'There's a reason for asking?'

'At the moment, there is none, but I have always found it is the question I do not ask which turns out to be the one I should.'

'It's an Opel.'

'Is it a saloon?'

'An estate.'

'And what is its colour?'

'Green.'

'Then thank you for your kind patience, Señora, Señor. Good afternoon. Or should I say, Good evening?'

Locke tried to speak facetiously. 'As we've enjoyed a drink, it has to be evening. No Englishman would consider drinking in the afternoon.'

Alvarez left. The interior of his car was burning hot despite the lowered windows and as he switched on the fan, beads of sweat began to prickle his cheeks and neck. The Lockes were probably sweating even harder, but not because of the heat.

Thirteen

When driving to the post on Tuesday morning, traffic forced Alvarez to a halt when abreast of Garaje Tomeu. He stared at the grey Opel Vectra in the show window and in his imagination ordered a similar car with air-conditioning . . . In the strange way in which a mind could work, he suddenly realized that when he had told Salas it would be next to impossible to prove the negative, he had overlooked something . . . But Salas, alarmed at the consequences of tangling with a politician, had forbade him to pursue any further enquiries into the possible destination of the money in Muir's safe. He had had reason. There was nothing which, on the face of things, remotely connected Muir's death with the sale of the Wilderness for development, so there could be no justification for pursuing any inquiry – doubly so, when there was that prominent politician threatening to breathe fire . . . He had to forget the Wilderness and its future, however reluctant he was to do so. Indeed, it was absurd to imagine that anything he could say or do might ever have the slightest effect . . .

The traffic moved once more.

He was certain Locke's alibi was false. Laura had been so frightened on her husband's behalf, she had invented the visit – to the obvious consternation of her husband. The Marshes must be questioned to expose the falsity of that alibi.

Tabitha had been at Muir's house on the Saturday and so her evidence should be useful, even if only in negative mode. Jemima Muir and Grant had had a bitter row with Muir. Assume she had threatened Muir that if he did not give her money, she would bring an action against him in the English courts since he still owned property in London. At which point, the pleasure of making a fool of her had inadvisably led him to say that the property was in the process of being sold and by the time she could get the law moving, the money would be abroad, out of reach of any court; further, he had added that his entire estate would go to a foundation when he died . . . Nothing could have been clearer than that only his early death could bring any benefit to her. She had known the danger to him of any wound . . .

He found a parking space in the shade, but did not climb out of the car and make his way to the post. As would any efficient detective, he had identified which facts were germane to the case and which were not; as would any efficient detective, he had decided to pursue the first and forget the second. Emotion must never play a part in any investigation . . . Yet when stopped in front of Garaje Tomeu, he had identified a possibility he had overlooked; true, totally irrelevant to the case in hand, so there could be no excuse for following it up . . . Yet one could claim that loose ends should always be tied up, however apparently irrelevant, to make certain they were no longer loose. And it wouldn't be as if he were shirking work; indeed, he would be adding to his work . . .

Elena met him in the hall of Sa Rotaga. 'I was going to phone to say I've finished the list,' she said.

He tried to work out what she was talking about.

Her expression sharpened. 'You asked me to write down all the names of the señor's guests I could remember. I thought it was important; it obviously was not.'

'On the contrary, it's very important, but I've so much to worry about that just for a moment, I couldn't place what list it was.'

'You don't need a memory in your job?'

'Normally, it's a hundred and one per cent . . . I've been waiting for the list because it's so vital to my investigation.'

'You are suggesting it has taken me too long? Perhaps you expected me to drop all my other work to do what you wanted?'

Dolores could not have bettered the way in which she had twisted his words to imply he was a typical selfish, unthinking male. 'Of course I didn't expect that . . . If I might have the list?' he asked meekly.

'It's in my handbag.'

He followed her into the kitchen, where she crossed to one of the working surfaces on which was a black handbag. She opened this, brought out a sheet of notepaper, but did not immediately hand it to him. 'I spent a great deal of time on this. And Lorenzo demanded to know who I was writing to.'

'Did you explain it was police work?'

'You think I was going to keep that a secret so that he became really annoyed?'

'Of course not.'

'A good husband will always be suspicious.'

'And a wife has the right—'

'You are about to try to tell me how a good wife should behave?'

He lacked the nerve. 'May I see the list now?'

She handed it to him. A quick glance was sufficient to

convince him it was going to be of little use. Of the several people listed, only two had surnames. 'I am very grateful; very grateful indeed.'

'So you should be.'

'And please assure your husband—'

'I will decide what to say to him.'

He gave up. 'Is Pablo here today?'

'You imagine he stayed at home because there is no one but me to see that he isn't here?'

'Of course I don't think any such thing. Where will I find him?'

'You would not expect him to be in the garden?'

He crossed to the outside door.

'I am about to prepare merienda for Pablo and me. Do you want some?'

One moment as sharp as a cactus thorn, the next honey-tongued. How could any man hope to keep abreast of a woman's moods? He had had his merienda in Llueso, but it would have been ungracious to refuse her offer. 'That would be great.'

He left the house and crossed the lawn to where Ortiz was hunkered down, replacing the plug of a motor mower. 'Trouble?' he asked.

'It's never anything else with this bloody machine.' Ortiz gave the box spanner one last twist, replaced the lead, stood. 'It's clapped out. I told the señor so many times and said I needed a new mower because this one was wasting his time and money. He wouldn't have it. Said he couldn't afford to buy a new one.'

'The rich try never to spend their own money, only other people's.'

'He spent when he wanted to. You don't think he enjoyed the women for free, do you?'

'I hope not or the world's an even more unequal place

than I thought . . . There's something I want to ask you, but Elena says she's getting merienda, so it can wait.'

They made their way to the kitchen. On a plate on the table was a round coca. There were several ways to a woman's heart. But only one that could be guaranteed never to fail. As he sat, Alvarez said, 'That looks really delicious, which means you cooked it.'

'You think I would serve a bought coca when I have the time to make one?' She cut a large slice and put this on a plate which she passed to him. He ate a mouthful. 'Sweeter and softer than a maiden's kiss!'

'Why d'you think the señor liked it so much?' Ortiz asked. 'Not that the likes of his women had been maidens for many years.'

'Don't speak ill of the dead,' she snapped.

'The women are still alive.'

'But he, may the Good Lord have mercy on his damaged soul, is not.'

'Then tell me—'

'It would be better if you let your tongue rest.'

The coffee machine hissed and she switched off the gas, used an oven cloth to lift it and pour coffee into the three mugs on the table.

Alvarez helped himself to sugar and milk, stirred the coffee, drank. He hoped there would be an offer of the traditional brandy, then remembered Ortiz didn't drink. He ate more coca by way of consolation. 'What I've come to ask is, did the señor use a local garage to have his car serviced and repaired and if so, which one?'

'It's that place in Playa Neuva which sells real expensive jobs, but I can't remember its name,' Ortiz answered.

'Garaje Epsa,' Elena said.

'How d'you know that?' Ortiz asked, piqued she could answer.

'Because my Cousin Eduardo owns it.'

'I never knew that.'

'You think I tell you everything?'

'Mostly, you tell me nothing.'

'Because a loose tongue causes more trouble than a loose shoe.'

'If you're suggesting—'

Alvarez hastened to bring the bickering to an end. 'Garaje Epsa is in Playa Neuva?'

'Port Playa Neuva,' she corrected. 'When Cousin Eduardo heard where I was working, he said the señor bought his car and had it serviced there; he also said the señor acted like he thought himself the greatest hidalgo in the land. As I told Cousin Eduardo, if he thought he'd cause to complain, he should do my job. Working for a man who never thought of anyone but himself, had no modesty, and enjoyed all the vices a decent woman knows nothing about.'

'Then how do you know what he was enjoying?' Ortiz asked.

She sniffed loudly.

'And who's speaking ill of the dead this time?'

'To tell the truth is not to speak ill.'

Alvarez ate his last mouthful of coca, looked at the portion left on the plate in the centre of the table.

'Do you want some more?' she asked.

'Just for once, I would; it's quite the most delicious I've ever tasted.' Had Dolores asked him for an opinion, he would naturally have said, almost as good as the coca she made. Women resented comparisons which did not favour themselves.

Port Playa Neuva was at the eastern end of a twenty-kilometre sweep of sand, the finest beach on the island.

From the port, ferries sailed to Menorca and other destinations, small cargo ships brought oil for the power station, cars and general cargo from the Peninsula; in the marina, the large number of sail and power boats testified to the wealth of some who visited or lived on the island.

Garaje Epsa, in a prime position on the front, was not for the parsimonious motorist; in the large showroom were a Jaguar and a Mercedes. Alvarez climbed the short flight of stairs to the lushly furnished office where a young secretary – frizzy hair, tight blouse, short skirt, arch manner – said Cousin Eduardo was in Germany, attending a conference, and Santiago, the manager, was visiting a potential client and she'd no idea how long he would be away since Belgians were always such difficult customers.

Alvarez said he'd return later. It was far too hot to walk anywhere, so he sat at one of the shaded tables at the first café he reached, reluctantly accepting he would have to pay twice as much for a coffee and a brandy as he would two or three roads back from the front.

He stared out at the passing crowds, the harbour, and the bay. He could remember when there had been only the sea, sand, pine trees, solitude . . . and poverty. Why did life so seldom grant a benefit which came unencumbered?

When he returned to the garage, Santiago was there. 'I'm very busy, so you'll have to hurry it.' He opened a file on the highly polished desk.

The epitome of a luxury car salesman, Alvarez decided – expensive linen suit, a tie featuring a formless explosion of colour, black hair smoothed down, a neat little moustache, and a supercilious manner. 'I understand Señor Muir was one of your clients?'

'Why do you say "was"?'

'You have not heard that he died?'

'When?'

'Just over a week ago.'

'What bad luck!'

Commiseration was surely for the garage, not Muir. 'I'm having to make enquiries following his death and one of the facts I need to know is, roughly six weeks ago, did he bring a wheel in to have a puncture mended?'

'I have no idea.'

'You keep work records?'

'Of course.'

'Then you can check them and find out.'

Santiago hesitated, reluctantly stood and crossed to a second, much smaller office in which the secretary worked. When he returned, he sat down, fiddled with a pencil, said: 'Why do you want to know?'

'The answer could be important.'

'How?'

'If it is important, you'll find out.'

Santiago briefly looked at him, his expression bad tempered, then turned as the secretary stepped into the office. 'He didn't have a puncture mended here. Not what was put down in the books, anyway.'

'If work was done, it would have been recorded,' he said hurriedly, worried Alvarez might imagine that the figures presented to the tax officials were not comprehensively correct.

As the secretary left, Alvarez said: 'I suppose it's very possible he left the wheel somewhere else for the repair?'

'Most unlikely. We strongly advised him to have all work to his car carried out here so that he could be certain it was done skilfully.'

'Repairing a puncture doesn't exactly call for unusual skill.'

Santiago shrugged his shoulders.

The normal owner usually favoured a particular garage

– often the one where he bought the car – in the belief work would be more quickly and carefully carried out. So there could now be reason to accept Muir's car had not suffered a puncture and Vives's story was nonsense. Yet to be certain would need every garage in the area to be questioned and that would be a long and exhausting task; and what defined the 'area'? Muir might have driven anywhere on the island after the puncture and have handed the wheel to one of the businesses which offered immediate repair . . . Common sense and practical considerations confirmed that, lacking evidence to the contrary, Vives had been lying in an effort to explain why his phone number had been written down in the guide book. He had lied because the truth was dangerous to himself and others . . .

He thanked Santiago – a waste of good manners – and left. Seated in his car, he checked the time and found it was still too early to go home for lunch. When he returned to the office, Salas might well phone and ask where he'd been and what he'd been doing. Since he dare not admit he had been disobeying orders, he needed a cover. And if that called for some work, so be it. Elena had provided two surnames. What better justification for an absence from the office than that he had been questioning one of the persons concerned?

He had names, but no addresses. The simplest way of finding these out was surely to call in at a bar and request to see their telephone directory.

Fourteen

Nearer to the port than to Llueso, Urbanizacíon Cielo was set out in four levels on the side of a hill. Almost every property had a good view of the bay and each had cost considerably more than it would have done had it been built on level ground. For Mallorquins, this willingness to pay for something as unproductive as a view was one of the more inexplicable traits of the foreigners.

Ca'n Epan, on the second of the four roads, was a small bungalow of typically awkward shape. It lay some five metres below the level of the road and the drive down was steep enough to worry Alvarez. Little attempt had been made to create a garden, hardly surprising in view of the slope, the stoniness of the soil, and the several large outcrops of rock.

He rang the bell to the side of the front door; after a while, he rang again.

The door finally opened. 'Do you expect me to run?' Adela asked aggressively, in rapid, grammatically incorrect, but comprehensible Spanish.

Her heavily jowled face, sharp nose, veined cheeks, generous girth, and lack of dress sense, reminded him of an ancient aunt who, when he was young, had insisted on hugging him until he had been terrified he was about to suffocate amidst her extensive bosom. 'Indeed no, Señora . . .' he began in English.

'Señorita. Who are you and what do you want?'

'Inspector Alvarez of the Cuerpo General de Policia. I am conducting the investigation into the unfortunate death of Señor Muir—'

'Then why waste your time coming here?'

'You may be able to help me.'

'A ridiculous suggestion.'

'But if you knew him, you may be able to tell me something about him.'

'What's that supposed to mean?'

'I need to understand what kind of a man he was . . .'

'He can be summed up in one word. A typical cad. You won't appreciate the nuances, of course. Indeed, many English these days wouldn't either since caddishness has become almost normal . . . Unless you intend to stand there for the rest of the morning, you'd better come through. And you'll want a drink, of course.'

'It's not necessary . . .'

'Since when has a Mallorquin drunk only out of necessity?'

Bewildered by her manner, he closed the front door, followed her through a plainly furnished sitting room, notable only for a large oil painting on one wall. 'My father,' she said, as she noticed his quick glance, 'served in the army all his life, wounded twice in the war, decorated, and finally awarded a pension that just kept him out of penury. Your country honours you when it needs you, forgets you when it doesn't; always been the same.' She stepped out on to a balcony, edged with wrought-iron railings, on which were a table and four white patio chairs. 'Can't see you in the army,' she said, surveying his slack form with disapproval.

He carefully kept as far as possible from the edge of the balcony; the drop beyond probably was not all that great, but due to his altophobia, it gained the frightening presence of an abyss. 'As a matter of fact, Señorita, I was in the army.'

'Presumably, you're talking about your time as a conscript? No connexion whatsoever with a proper army. What do you want to drink?'

Her sudden change of subject left his mind trailing and it was several seconds before he said: 'May I have a brandy with just ice?'

She picked up an empty glass from the table and returned inside. He sat. The bungalow stood high enough to afford a broad view of the bay and surrounding mountains and because of distance, existing development was stripped of much of its ugliness; even so, the blocks of tourist accommodation in the Wilderness were visual scars. Were Doña Terrasa unwittingly to sell her land because of trusting her nephew, then further scars would turn into a visual abomination . . .

Adela returned, put two glasses down on the table, sat; the chair briefly creaked. 'So he did the decent thing, for once, and shot himself.'

'He was not shot.'

'That's what people have been saying.'

'They are wrong.'

'They usually are.'

'He received an injury which caused internal bleeding that would not stop and as a consequence became so weak he fell into the swimming pool and, lacking the strength to save himself, drowned.'

'Why didn't the woman fish him out?'

'What woman?'

'How would I know?'

'But you can be certain someone was with him when he fell into the pool?'

'What the devil are you getting at?'

'From the way you've been speaking, I gathered you knew what happened.'

'My dear man, of course I don't.' She drank eagerly.

'You were not there?'

'Never went near the place unless it was a party.'

'Then you are assuming he was with a woman?'

'Hardly a difficult presumption to make.'

'In fact, he did entertain that day, but she left in the late afternoon.'

'By which time, he'd had all he wanted from her.'

Her words surprised him and even vaguely shocked him. A naive reaction, he accepted. She might be an elderly spinster, but she was no ingénue; added to which, the drink she had just finished was clearly not her first of the day. 'How well did you know Señor Muir?'

'An impossible question to answer.'

'Why is that?'

'How can one be certain how much there is to know? What do you mean by "know"? The Bible has a different connotation to normal social life. Are you asking me if I could judge how he'd react to circumstances? Did I understand his attitudes? Would I trust him? The answer to that last is, never.'

'Did you often meet him?'

'I've said, at his grand parties. Unless he was trying to impress, he'd no time to waste on an old woman like me.'

'Would you think he was popular amongst the foreigners?'

'Which foreigners?'

'People like yourself . . .'

'I am English, not a foreigner,' she snapped.

'Señorita, since you are living in Spain—'

'Which has nothing to do with it.'

Only a brave man stepped into the plaza de torros whilst a fighting bull was pawing the sand. 'Would you consider he was generally popular?'

'Of course not. If you're wealthy, that's unlikely; if you're a cad, that's impossible.'

'So there must have been many who disliked him and some, perhaps, who even hated him?'

'Almost certainly.'

'Have you heard anyone express such a hatred?'

'There are people who have said hard things about him and jealousy always sounds very bitter. Of course, when Laura and Keir were so upset and angry at the party, I did wonder . . .' She stood. 'Don't you want another drink?'

He drained his glass, handed it to her. After she had gone indoors, he stared out at the bay, a distant circle of blue shot with reflected sunlight. To the right there rose a thin column of smoke – someone was burning rubbish, contrary to the law at this time of the year. A nearby dog began to bark and a more distant one accepted the challenge. A kestrel swooped into view, hovered, disappeared. A rustle by his side caught his attention and he watched a gecko climb a concrete pillar with zig-zag motion that kept its tail sweeping from side to side.

She returned, handed him his glass, sat.

'Señorita, you mentioned people called Laura and Keir who were at a party and for some reason became angry and upset . . . Was this because of something Señor Muir had said or done?'

'I do not indulge in idle gossip.'

'I am trying to understand the kind of person Señor Muir was and why someone should dislike him sufficiently to wish to kill or, at the very least, injure him. Anything I am told is not gossip, it is information necessarily given to help me learn the truth . . . Is Keir a Christian name?'

'Of course.'

'What is his surname?'

'Locke.'

'Who is Laura?'

'His wife.'

'Señor and Señora Locke heard something at the party which surprised and angered them?'

'Can you assure me on your honour – I will assume you understand what that means – this is something you must know?'

'Indeed I can.'

'I was talking to Laura, Keir, and . . .Who were the other couple? . . . Of course, the Reeds. Pleasant people unless he has had too much to drink and then his background becomes apparent. Always the same, isn't it?'

'What is?'

'Background will out.'

'Was it something Señor or Señora Reed said which upset Señor Locke?'

'Why should you think it was?'

'Since you mentioned them, I supposed they were of some importance.'

'Of considerable unimportance.'

'Then I don't understand.'

'You are obviously very uncertain of yourself. Not much good at your job?'

'I imagine my superior chief would say not.'

'At least that's honest! Drink up.'

He emptied his glass.

'Pass it to me.' She carried the two glasses out of the room, returned with them refilled, handed him his, sat.

'Señorita, who said or did whatever it was which so disturbed the Lockes?'

'I've already told you.'

'I don't think you mentioned any details. You were about to do so, but then became interested in the Reeds . . .'

'They do not interest me. Pleasant enough – when he's sober – but not exactly . . . Do you understand what I mean?'

'I don't think so.'

'Hardly surprising. You Mallorquins lack the opportunity to appreciate the subtleties of social distinctions.'

'Who said or did—?'

'Must you keep asking the same question?'

'Only until I receive an answer.'

'You have an arrogant manner.'

'I'm sorry you should think so.'

'I'm quite certain you don't give a damn . . . It was something I said.'

'Which was what?'

'I told them I'd met the . . .What is their name?'

'Reed?'

'Why do you keep mentioning them?'

'I thought . . . Señorita, I am confused.'

'You obviously have a far smaller capacity for alcohol than most of your compatriots.' She drank, replaced the glass on the table; two beads of gin and tonic on her incipient moustache glinted in the sun. 'The Noyeses. There's talk he ran into business troubles back in England and had to leave in a hurry. One has to say he has that kind of appearance.'

'You told the Reeds about the Noyeses . . .'

'For God's sake, forget them. I mentioned to Keir and the others that I'd met Valerie Noyes, who'd told me she'd met . . . Sounds like Consequences, don't you think?'

126

'Consequences?'

'It's extraordinary how little you Mallorquins know about the outside world. No doubt you never even played sardines when you were young. Of course, it was an innocent game in the old days. I imagine that now the efficient hostess never suggests it's played unless she can offer a sufficient number of condoms.'

'Señorita, would you tell me what Valerie Noyes said to you.'

'She'd met this woman and her boyfriend in a shop . . . People who were having an affair used to try their best to hide that fact, nowadays, they have no hesitation in broadcasting the fact. There's no taste these days, is there?'

'Perhaps not. Then you—'

'The old values are laughed at, but they made for a more regulated society. Hypocrisy can be a virtue as well as a vice.'

'Valerie Noyes . . .'

She drained her glass. 'Still not drinking?'

'I need a clear head if I am to follow what you tell me.'

'The ability to hold his liquor was the mark of a gentleman.' She stood, had suddenly to grip the top of a chair to hold her balance. 'Well, are you going to give me your glass?'

'Señorita, if perhaps you could tell me what happened before we have another drink?'

'No capacity; no gentleman.' She sat with more force than intended and momentum would have sent the chair crashing had not Alvarez managed to reach out and support it until she was settled. 'Bloody legs are unsteady,' she said angrily. 'Mallorquin carpentry.'

'You told Señor Locke you'd met Valerie Noyes, who, I think, said she'd met someone?'

'Dinty. Are you sure you don't want another drink? . . .

When a man joined his regiment, they used to get him drunk to understand his real character; in vino veritas. Nothing truer.'

'Dinty is a name?'

'I'm told it's a common nickname for someone called Muir. It's very difficult to understand why. Do you know?'

'No, Señorita.'

'You Mallorquins are surprisingly ignorant.'

'Was it the name, Dinty, which upset Señor Locke?'

'That's what I've just said.'

'He appeared to be angry?'

'And disturbed. So disturbed, they both left soon afterwards and without eating anything. Do you have to be told everything time after time?'

'Did he explain why it affected him so much?'

'No.'

'Then you've no idea why the name had this effect?'

'Not specifically, but . . .'

'Yes?'

'You understand how much I dislike gossip?'

'That is very obvious.'

'There was a rumour soon after they came to live here that their daughter had committed suicide in unfortunate circumstances. It makes one wonder if the circumstances were of a certain nature, remembering how the name, Dinty, so upset them. Scott's never left the women alone, so I have to confess I wouldn't be surprised if . . . You follow what I'm telling you?'

'I hope so.'

'Money can corrupt even those from fairly good backgrounds . . . It doesn't matter what anyone says, background is the rock on which a good society rests. That's why you Mallorquins have so much to learn about cultured living.'

'It is true that we often find it difficult to understand the behaviour of many tourists.'

'What's that? Are you trying to be a smart-arse?' she demanded angrily.

'Life has taught me the futility of such an ambition.' He stood. 'Thank you for your help.'

'Why can't you sit still for more than five minutes?'

'I have to return home.'

'You need another drink before you go.'

'I think not, thank you, or perhaps I would fail to arrive.'

'No capacity, that's your trouble!'

The family was eating lunch.

Dolores's tone was frosty. 'We waited for you for as long as was possible.'

'That was very kind—' Alvarez began.

'But I was not going to have the meal, over which I had spent hours slaving in the kitchen, ruined just because you could not be bothered to return home at the right time.'

He sat. 'I had to question someone and that proved a much more difficult task than I'd expected. She was drinking heavily and so it took a long time to persuade her to tell me what I wanted to know.'

'And, no doubt, even longer for you to understand when she did.'

'If you're suggesting I've been drinking heavily, the fact is, I had a couple and then refused another.'

She spooned Arroz a la Marinera on to a plate. 'As my mother often said, "The more ridiculous the lie, the more ashamed is the man."' She passed him the plate. 'However, I doubt you suffer even a twinge of shame when speaking such unbelievable nonsense.'

Fifteen

'Yes?' said the secretary with the plum-laden voice.

'Inspector Alvarez, Señorita. I should like to speak to the superior chief.'

'Wait.'

He slumped back in the chair, receiver cradled against his ear. It seemed hotter than ever and the fan did little to assuage the discomfort. Man was most certainly not made to work in such conditions . . .

'Yes?' said Salas.

'Señor, I am ringing for permission to ask the authorities in England to make certain enquiries in connexion with the death of Señor Muir.'

'Why?'

'I have very recently learned that one of the major suspects may have had a motive for his death.'

'You have considered someone to be a major suspect before you even know he had a motive for the killing?'

'That is because—'

'You regard logic as irrelevant.'

'Because it is probable Señor Locke was seen driving his car towards Sa Rotaga shortly after five o'clock on the Saturday afternoon.'

'Will you ever learn to make a report in proper order?' Salas demanded angrily.

'I was about to explain—'

'Since your explanations are even more confusing than that which you are trying to explain, just detail the motive for the killing.'

'I don't know.'

'Even after many years, you retain the capacity to astonish me with your incompetence.'

'Señor, I may not know, but I can guess. There was a rumour—'

'You offer me a guess based on a rumour. Was the rumour conceived in a crystal ball?'

'There is a possibility that Señor Locke's daughter committed suicide some time in the past. When Señor and Señora Locke were at the party given by Señor Muir on the Wednesday before his death, the name "Dinty" was mentioned to them and this seemed to upset both of them so much they left the party very shortly afterwards.'

'Did they say anything to indicate a direct connexion between the name and their leaving?'

'I don't think so.'

'Then it is mere presumption there was one.'

'Señor Locke was described as angry and disturbed. And they left before they ate anything.'

'Why should that fact hold any significance?'

Alvarez wondered how Salas could be so stupid? Who was going to forgo what must have been a delicious meal except for some overwhelming reason? '"Dinty" is the nickname for people called Muir. To hear it used with reference to Señor Muir must have immediately raised in their minds the possibility that he might have been connected with their daughter's death.'

'I fail to understand why, if it's a common nickname.'

'Young women can become dangerously emotional in a relationship and it's obvious Señor Muir had all the techniques.'

'Techniques for what?'

'Pursuing women. Which is why I want to ask England—'

'Once again, you prove yourself incapable of conducting an investigation without seeking to introduce the subject of sex.'

'Señor, as I think I have said before, sex is often present in a relationship.'

'And as I have certainly said before, only in those of a certain nature.'

'Their reaction to hearing the name would be explained if their daughter had had a torrid affair with Muir and they blamed him for her death.'

'Have you consulted a doctor?'

'About what, Señor?'

'The fact you suffer from satyriasis. I imagine the medical profession would regard you as presenting a text-book paradigm for the disease.' He cut the connexion.

Disease. A word to send shivers down the spine. It wasn't life that was so extraordinary, it was the fact that one wasn't yet dead. The air that one breathed was laden with germs, food could poison; to shake hands was to risk a fatal infection . . . He stood, hurried downstairs to the general room. The only cabo present said: 'What brings you to a working area?'

'Is there a dictionary here?'

'What would we want one for? Come to that, what can you possibly want one for?'

'I need to find out what I may be suffering from.'

'Overweight, enlarged liver, fumed-up lungs . . .'

Alvarez left and went along the corridor to the brigada's room, which was empty. In the glass-fronted cabinet were several seldom read books detailing Guardia Civil rules, regulations, and procedures, a shelf of legal tomes, and a dictionary. This last detailed satyriasis as an excessive sexual desire in men. Greatly relieved to discover the superior chief had merely been responding to his own excessively prudish standards, Alvarez returned upstairs, sat, opened the bottom right-hand drawer of the desk, brought out bottle and glass, poured himself a heavy drink. A man needed to celebrate when he learned death was not yet reaching out to enfold him in its embrace.

After a second drink, he pondered the question. Did he have permission to contact the English police and ask them to find out if Locke's daughter had committed suicide and, if so, had known Muir? To phone Salas again could only ensure more trouble. It must be reasonable to assume that since permission had not been specifically refused, there had been the intention to grant it.

Requests for co-operation with foreign forces were supposed to be passed through Interpol, but that meant bureaucratic delay. Not many months before, there had been a case in which a British suspect had fled to the island; Barry Denton had flown over and he had been detailed to work with the other. As the old Mallorquin maxim said: If you help shear your neighbour's sheep, you can expect him to help shear yours.

He checked in the notebook in which he listed frequently used or personally relevant telephone numbers, found Denton's, tapped this out on the phone.

Dolores was in the kitchen and, to judge from the sounds, washing up, so Jaime poured himself another brandy; he passed the bottle across the table to Alvarez. 'I saw Mauricio again this afternoon.'

'What's he doing this end of the island?'

'Came to see his sister, who's been ill.'

Alvarez refilled his glass. 'What's wrong with her?'

'Mauricio didn't say except she seems worn out through working too hard.'

There was a call from the kitchen. 'With a husband as lazy as Ricardo, what else can be expected?'

Alvarez tried, with a shake of the head, to dissuade Jaime from responding, but was ignored.

'That's not fair. Ricardo has a good job.'

'For a man, a good job is one in which he has very little to do.'

'Doesn't he provide her with a nice home?'

Dolores came through the bead curtain with sufficient momentum to send the strings of beads noisily clashing against each other. She folded her arms over her bosom, an attitude made pugnacious by the long-bladed knife in her right hand. 'And like all men, believes that is more than enough.'

'What else can she expect?'

'A woman soon learns to expect little, however much she wants. Of what use is it to expect a husband who arrives home and does not complain endlessly about how hard he has striven all day; who is not so exhausted he must sit and rest while his wife slaves in the kitchen to prepare a meal which he will gulp down without a thought to her suffering; who, despite declared exhaustion, does not find the energy to refill his glass many times before, during, and after the meal?' She unwrapped her arms, causing the knife to scythe the air, returned through the bead curtain into the kitchen.

'Why's she always getting at me?' Jaime asked in a low voice.

'You did rather lead into it,' Alvarez replied.

'How?'

'By arguing.'

'You're saying I shouldn't tell her when she's talking nonsense?'

'If you didn't, you'd find life more peaceful.'

'She doesn't understand.'

'Understanding is not one of their virtues.'

'Have they any?'

'It is to be hoped some have . . . And that others haven't.'

After a while, Jaime understood and sniggered. 'Like Natalie used to—' He came to a sudden stop.

'Used to spread her favours wide?'

'How would I know?' Jaime stared at the bead curtain, his expression uneasy. As there was no comment from the kitchen, he relaxed, drank, said: 'Did you know Mauricio is working for the government these days?'

'Can't say I did.'

'That's how he heard about the Wilderness coming up for sale.'

'You said you couldn't remember who'd told you.'

'But I do now . . . Always was a moaner, was Mauricio; complained about something all the time we were in the Bar Espanol—' He stopped, looked at the bead curtain.

'What's he got to complain about if he's working for the government – he'll be paid twice for doing half.'

'Says he can only just afford to live with prices going up because of the euro. And there's his boss buying one of those Jaguar cars that cost a fortune and talking about moving into a bigger house.'

Alvarez had raised his glass to drink; he put it down on the table. 'Which department does Mauricio work in?'

'Can't say exactly; something to do with housing from the way he was talking.'

'Do you know the boss's name?'

'He did mention it.'

'What was it?'

'Yague. Doesn't sound Mallorquin, does it?'

'And his Christian name?'

'Mauricio just called him Bastard Yague.'

'I wonder if it starts with a V?'

'And if it does?'

'Then perhaps . . . But catch the pigeon before you decide how to eat it.'

'Who's catching pigeons? Anyway, you know I don't like 'em ever since I had one that was bad.'

On Wednesday, Alvarez arrived in the kitchen before Dolores had made the hot chocolate. She stared at him. 'I haven't called you, yet you're down here!'

'I've some very important work to do.'

'And you are in this much of a hurry to do it? What kind of work?'

'For the moment, it's very confidential.'

She sniffed loudly. 'You think I wish to pry?'

He assured her he did not. He explained that his investigation had to be conducted in total secrecy because should word about it escape, there would be disaster.

'And naturally you do not trust me to keep my mouth closed?' she said with haughty anger.

'It's not like that. To tell the truth, I'm really scared because of what I know or suspect and I wouldn't want you . . . When a sprat is in danger of getting in the way of a shark . . .'

'It turns away.'

'And if it can, but it can't?'

'I don't understand.'

'Neither do I, really. Can it possibly matter that much?'

'Can what matter?'

'The loss of something priceless yet which cannot be given a commercial value.'

'If you can only speak in meaningless riddles, it will be better if you say nothing.' She banged the saucepan on

136

the stove to indicate annoyance, poured into it the milk to make the hot chocolate.

Alvarez sat at his desk and wondered how big a fool he was being? While there was great profit to be made from developing, there would be development; perhaps only a very few could perceive beauty in wild land; an honest politician was a contradiction in terms . . . And yet wasn't there still room in the world for fools?

He dialled the office of the Minister for Sustainable Development. The woman who answered his call spoke in a manner similar to the superior chief's secretary, raising the interesting question, did work fashion attitude? 'Would you be kind enough to tell me the full name of the minister?'

She pointed out that the department was not an information bureau, the staff were overworked, and details were on record . . . 'Valeriano Carlos Yague,' she snapped, before she rang off.

VY. The initials on the two bundles of notes which totalled six hundred thousand euros. Coincidence? Mauricio had told Jaime that his boss was considering moving into a bigger house, having bought a large and expensive car. More coincidences?

He rang Traffic and asked to be given the names of all owners of Jaguar cars bought in the past six months.

'That's one hell of a job!'

'Surely not with computers?'

'You know more about it than I do?'

'Of course not.'

'Then suppose you don't suggest how easy it's going to be to spend hours searching the records when we're grossly overworked as it is. What's the justification for the request?'

Unless the concocted justification was emotionally strong,

there was every reason to believe his request would be put on one side until someone could perhaps be bothered to deal with it. 'We've had a hit-and-run and the only identification is a large Jaguar, maybe grey in colour. A woman was walking her young child across the road and the car came round the corner so quickly the driver couldn't stop, lost control, and mowed 'em both down, then took off, leaving 'em lying there.'

'There's only one thing good enough for his kind – the garotte. OK. We'll get you the names just as soon as we can call 'em up. By the way, why restrict cars bought in the last six months?'

Because that generously covered the period when the bank records from Muir's safe showed the first large sum of money in cash had been withdrawn. 'The eyewitness who identified the make said there was a small modification which shows it could not have been built before then.'

'Must have eyes like a hawk. So why didn't he get the number?'

And why did the man at the other end of the line keep asking questions? 'You know how irrational people can become. Said he didn't think of doing that until the car was too far away.'

'There's one born every minute. And most of 'em end up in the Cuerpo.' The speaker laughed.

The call over, Alvarez congratulated himself on his quick thinking as he checked the time. A little early to leave for his merienda. He considered the case in hand. There surely was more point to questioning the Marshes after he'd heard from England rather than before; their evidence should tell him whether to question the Lockes again; Jemima Muir's and Grant's alibi must be tested; he must have a word with Ortiz's wife; Tabitha might have learned something relevant . . . He'd talk to her after merienda.

Sixteen

Hotel Terramar dated back to the time when Puerto Llueso – as it was then called, Castilian being obligatory and Mallorquin forbidden – had consisted of a few large houses along the front, summer homes for wealthy persons from Palma and the Peninsula, two other small hotels which did not offer, let alone supply, luxury, and many fishermen's cottages. Since the tourist invasion, the hotel had twice been enlarged, each time without regard to visual harmony, so that it was now a hotchpotch of a building, yet it retained character, something many more modern hotels lacked.

The front road had been turned into a traffic-free walkway; Alvarez drove up it and parked. He crossed the creeper entwined, columned patio and once inside, went over to the reception desk where he introduced himself and explained he wanted a word with Señorita Telfer.

'I haven't seen her this morning, so I'll find out if she's in her room.' Adolfo – middle aged, beginning to bald, face expressing the sad acceptance of human nature which came from years of dealing with tourists – used the internal phone. After a moment, he replaced the receiver. 'She's not up there, so she's probably on the beach with her friend.'

'Presumably, a female friend?'

'Yes, but how did you—' He came to an abrupt stop.

'I'd like a bit of a chat.'

'I'm sorry, but I can't keep talking to you or the manager will complain.'

'Then we'll go to a café and have a coffee without fear of your being worried by him.'

'I'm on duty.'

'There are two of you, so your mate can hold the fort for a while.'

'Carlos wouldn't take kindly to being left on his own.'

It was clear Adolfo was one of life's downtrodden. 'Tell him that Inspector Alvarez has ordered you to accompany him to assist in his investigations and it is an offence to raise any objection.'

Adolfo looked at him uncertainly, then moved along the counter and spoke to his companion. When he returned, he said: 'I can't be very long. There's a busload of tourists due soon.'

'We'll get you back in time.'

They walked the short distance to tables set outside the first of the cafés, sat in the shade of the sun umbrella. A sweating waiter took their order – to Alvarez's surprise, Adolfo refused a brandy to accompany the coffee because he never drank during working hours – hurried on to the next table. Alvarez stared across the road at the beach, the sunbathers, the limpid, poster-blue water, the yachts with sagging, wind-short sails, the motor cruiser leaving a creamy wake, and the far mountains. Bartolomé Llinas, the only recognized locally born poet, had written that what enabled a man to face life was the hope death would reveal Heaven to be Puerto Llueso – a sentiment far more coherent than his poetry.

'I don't understand what you want . . .' Adolfo became nervously silent.

Alvarez produced a pack of cigarettes and offered it; the other shook his head. He struck a match and lit a cigarette.

'I want to hear what you can tell me about Señorita Tabitha Telfer.'

'There's nothing to tell.'

'You never speak to her?'

'Yes, of course; sometimes. But never for long.'

'Is she friendly?'

'Very friendly.'

'I've been told she's attractive?'

'She's that all right,' Adolfo answered, with more force than he'd spoken before.

'And she's here with a friend. What do you know about her?'

'Nothing. Nothing really.'

'You make it sound as if that's not completely accurate.'

Adolfo was about to speak, checked his words when the waiter came up to the table, placed a small coffee cortado in front of each of them and a brandy next to Alvarez's cup and saucer, spiked the bill and left.

Alvarez opened an individual pack of sugar, emptied half of it into his cup, drank some brandy, then some coffee. 'You were going to tell me what you know and have heard about Tabitha and her friend,' he said, with sufficient certainty to make it seem that was true.

Adolfo stirred his coffee with a nervous compulsion. 'I . . . I normally never listen to gossip even though there's so much of it around in any hotel.'

'But you have heard something about them?'

'I shouldn't repeat it.'

'On the contrary, it's your duty to do so.'

'If the manager ever hears—'

'He'll learn nothing from me. So tell me what there is to tell.'

Adolfo increased his rate of stirring. 'Lucía – she's one

of the maids – says one morning she was behind in her work and when she came to their room, reckoned they'd be on the beach and didn't bother to knock, just unlocked the door and went in to make the beds. And . . . She says the way they were behaving, she reckoned they were . . . very interested in each other.'

'She's suggesting they're lezzies?'

'She couldn't think what was happening if . . . Well, if they weren't.'

'Then from what I've learned, she needs to improve her imagination.'

'I did say it was only a rumour.'

'Even a rumour needs a touch of possibility.' Alvarez drank the last of the brandy, called the waiter across and asked for another. As the waiter left, he said: 'Aren't the men around Tabitha all the time?'

'If they get the chance.'

'Don't you think that makes nonsense of her and her friend being a couple?'

'It's Lucía who thought—'

'Sure, but she was wrong. So now tell me anything else you can.'

The waiter returned, put a filled glass in front of Alvarez, picked up the empty one, spiked the second bill, left.

'What more is there to say?'

'There's nothing. In my job, there isn't time to get friendly with the guests and the manager doesn't like us doing that anyway.'

'He can't dictate your lives away from the hotel.'

'But he . . . Look, I've said good morning and maybe had a bit of a chat about how hot it is, but that's all. I'm married.'

Alvarez poured the brandy into the remaining coffee, drank that. 'You'll be wanting to get back to the hotel to meet the busload of tourists.' He picked up the spiked bills, read the totals, and had his worst fears confirmed. He left only a small tip. He stood. 'But before you do return, we'll have a quick walk along the beach for you to point out Tabitha to me.'

'I think I ought to hurry back—'

'Planes are always late and it's about time for the baggage handlers to go on strike again.'

Soon after stepping off the pavement on to the sand and walking between the dozens of sun-bathers, Adolfo said, 'There they are.'

Two men were talking to two women who sat on rush beach mats. The blonde, her bikini sufficiently abbreviated to leave only her most secret charms hidden, was smiling and returning the men's banter, her companion, slightly more covered, was staring out to sea, her expression bored. 'Señorita Tabitha Telfer is the blonde in the blue and red costume?' Alvarez asked.

'That's right.'

'Then thanks for your help.'

Adolfo took a step back towards the road, stopped. 'I was only saying what Lucía said . . .'

'I understand.'

'If the manager thought—'

'His thoughts won't receive any help from me.'

Adolfo left, far from reassured, Alvarez was certain. He studied the two men. Locals from their appearance and mannerisms. Cocksurely confident these foreign women would no more be able to resist their charm than all the others they had met during the summer; Tabitha seemed to be giving them encouragement – it was strange anyone so attractive should be bothered with two beach bums – her companion, none.

He walked around a stout lady who should have worn

a more enveloping costume, approached the group. 'Good morning,' he said in English.

The two men stared antagonistically at him and the larger, with a bodybuilder's physique, said to Tabitha in fractured English: 'You know?'

She shook her head.

He faced Alvarez and, identifying a fellow islander, suggested in colourful Mallorquin terms that he cleared off and found someone else to annoy.

'Cuerpo General de Policia.'

They were immediately uneasy, though not scared.

'So you can clear off, though perhaps not so awkwardly as you suggested I should.'

The larger man, determined to show aggression, said: 'You can't order us around.'

'You want to be arrested on suspicion of robbing tourists?'

'We haven't bloody robbed anyone.'

'I'm not bothered about details.'

'Come on,' said the second man nervously, 'let's move.'

'He's not busting things up.'

'Stay here and he'll nick us. For once get your brains back up to your head.' He turned away and began walking across the sand.

His companion scowled at Alvarez, muttered something unintelligible, finally followed his companion.

Tabitha took off her sunglasses and looked up at Alvarez. 'What was all that about?'

Until he had seen her eyes, he had thought it impossible there could be a deeper, more lustrous blue than the waters of the bay on a cloudless day. 'I'm sorry if you were disturbed by them, Señorita.'

'Amused, not disturbed.'

'What was so amusing about them?' Mary asked sharply.

'Watching them strut their stuff, thinking they were making an impression.'

'Of loutishness.'

He wondered if Mary's contempt was due in part at least to the fact they probably had been paying her little attention. On her own, many would find her fairly attractive – naturally wavy hair an unusual shade of brown, regular features, a body well shaped where that was an advantage – but in Tabitha's company she could only be second choice.

'Why did they leave?' Tabitha asked.

'I ordered them to go.'

'You ordered?'

'Yes, Señorita.'

'Then you're someone important?'

'An inspector in the Cuerpo General de Policia.' He realized after he'd spoken that he might just have sounded slightly pompous; almost as if he had been trying to impress her . . .

'A policeman! Did you threaten them with the Inquisition if they didn't do what you wanted?'

He smiled. 'That wasn't necessary.'

'Why did your order them away?'

'I wish to speak to you, Señorita . . .'

'What's your name?'

'Alvarez.'

'That doesn't sound like a Christian name.'

'It isn't.'

'Then what is that?'

She began to nibble the ends of her sunglasses. Normally, nothing could be less erotic, yet when she did that . . . 'Enrique. I'm afraid that what I have to discuss will probably distress you.'

'Then don't discuss it.'

'Unfortunately, I have to.'

'I hate being distressed.'

'You never are – it's always the other people,' Mary said.

'That's unkind.'

Mary smiled sarcastically as she picked up a handful of sand and let it trickle between her fingers.

'Señorita Tabitha . . .'

'You say that so sweetly. It makes me think . . . I'm not going to tell you what it makes me think.'

And he wasn't going to tell her what she made him think. 'I have to ask you about Señor Muir.'

'Why?'

'I am investigating the circumstances of his death.'

'The paper said he drowned.'

'That sadly is true, but he suffered two stab wounds before he fell into the swimming pool.'

'He was stabbed? Oh, my God!'

'Do you need smelling salts?' Mary asked.

'Don't be so beastly. It's a terrible shock to know it wasn't an accident and someone killed him . . . Enrique, surely you can't think I know anything about who did that?'

'Of course not.' Were her emotional responses genuine, or exaggerated in order to hold attention?

'She's far too squeamish to use a dagger,' Mary said. 'It would be different if he'd died from prussic acid.'

'How can you say such a terrible thing?' Tabitha asked plaintively.

Mary laughed.

It was going to be difficult, if not impossible, Alvarez decided, to question Tabitha if Mary, who seemed determined to needle her, were present. He asked Mary: 'Were you also friendly with Señor Muir?'

'Hardly, since he always took great care to ignore me.'

'Why d'you keep saying that?' Tabitha asked. 'More than once he invited you along, but you'd never go.'

'You think I'd enjoy watching you egging him on?'

'I do wish you wouldn't say things like that.'

'Then you shouldn't give me cause.'

Alvarez wondered what had caused Mary to be so aggressively bad tempered. 'Since you will seldom have been in his company, I don't think I need bother you.' He turned to Tabitha. 'Perhaps we might find somewhere more comfortable to talk?'

'Where do you suggest?'

'We could go to your hotel. The lounge will be cool,' he hastily added, for fear she thought he might be suggesting her bedroom.

'I don't really want to go indoors, out of the sun. I know what. There's a café just along the beach, so why don't we go there?'

He knew the café – touristy, charging even more exorbitant prices than the one he had only recently left. But if that was what she wanted . . .

She came to her feet in one easy movement. 'Lead on, Macduff.'

'Lay on,' corrected Mary sharply.

They walked along the sand, never far apart because of the need to wend their way between sunbathers, occasionally very close; at such moments . . . Did a man, he angrily asked himself, have to be buried before his mind calmed?

The café itself was on the shoreside of the path which ringed that part of the bay, the tables and chairs set out on the sand; through the centre of each table was the support for a large, very colourful sun umbrella. The sea reached within a couple of metres of the last table and that was where she chose to sit.

'Isn't it heaven?' she said.

It was. The beach, the three pine trees growing in the sand, the mill-pond sea, the surrounding mountains, the cloudless sky, and a young woman who would have made Botticelli paint a second *Birth of Venus* . . .

She moved her chair out of the shade of the umbrella and leaned back to gain the maximum amount of sunlight on her body. The thin straps of her minimal bikini top became strained and he wondered how much more pressure would be needed before they broke . . . Sweet Mary! Had there ever been such an absurdity? There he was, imagining a stolen glimpse of a bare breast when all about him were topless female sunbathers.

'Mary often says things she doesn't mean.'

'I rather gained that impression.'

'She gets a little peeved because . . .'

He was not surprised she did not finish the sentence. She had too sympathetic a nature to put the truth into words – when two women were together, men were always attracted to the prettier.

'She shocked me when she told me about Scott . . . I thought she was joking because she can have a cruel sense of humour, but then she showed me the article which described how he'd drowned in his swimming pool. I simply couldn't believe it because we'd been together until Saturday afternoon and it made me feel . . . I just can't think about it without being upset.'

'Of course not. And I'm very sorry I have to ask you about him.'

A young woman, dressed in a gaily patterned cotton frock, crossed the road and served the four who sat at the next table, then came up to them and, after a quick glance at Tabitha, said in reasonable English: 'What you wish to drink?'

Tabitha spoke to Alvarez. 'They serve daiquiris and I simply love them. Do you think I could have one?'

There was a price list, printed on pink paper, in a holder, but it was turned away from him and so he had no idea what a daiquiri – whatever that was – cost, beyond the fact it would be a remarkable number of euros. Prudence said that if his pocket was not to be emptied, he should content himself with a beer . . . But when was there room for prudence in the company of a lovely woman? 'And I'll have a Soberano with three cubes of ice.'

As the waitress left, Tabitha said: 'What are you going to ask me?'

'About the times you were with Señor Muir.'

'Why?'

'Because I need to learn more about him; because I must understand why, when you left his house, he told his gardener to drive you to your hotel.'

'How do you know he did?'

'I was told.'

'That's a bit . . . well, scary, that you should be interested. So what else have you learned about me?'

'Very little.'

'Ought I to be grateful for that?'

'I'm sure not.'

'How very diplomatic! Enrique, are you always solemn?'

'Am I being solemn?'

'As an owl.'

'How boring for you. I'm sorry. Blame it on my job.'

'You never relax when you're working?'

The waitress returned and put glasses down on the table, left.

Tabitha picked up her glass, looked at him across the

top of it. 'I'm certain you can be very unsolemn. So what are you like then?'

'I don't think I can answer. It needs someone else to do that.'

'That almost sounds like an invitation.'

For one wild moment, as her deep blue eyes gazed at him and he imagined she was hoping he would respond, he was about to claim that it was. But despite an overactive imagination, at the back of his mind there remained a small measure of common sense. She was every man's dream, he was a nearly middle-aged, far from successful detective. She smiled, moist lips slightly parted, and common sense began to slip. Perhaps he lacked youth, was not handsome or well built, but in place of such ephemeral assets, could he not offer the far more valuable ones of respect, sympathy, loyalty . . . ?

'I'm sorry, it obviously wasn't,' she said provocatively. She drank.

The moment had passed and he didn't know whether to be sad or sorry. 'Will you tell me how you first met Señor Muir?'

She didn't immediately answer, but said again how shocked she'd been when Mary had told her about his death. Perhaps the shock had been that much greater because of the manner in which they'd parted. Could he understand?

He assured her he could.

He wanted to know about their relationship, so she'd tell him, even though . . . She and Mary had gone into a bar and Scott had spoken to them with the easy confidence of sophisticated wealth. In no time, he'd invited them to dinner at one of his favourite restaurants. She'd said it would be fun, Mary had refused to go – so sharply, she had sounded rude. The restaurant had been fantastic. She couldn't remember its name or exactly where it was other than on top of a hill, or perhaps it was a mountain, and from it much of the island had been visible. There had been a very slight breeze to freshen the air as they sat out in the open; nightingales had sung in the woods which ringed the land just below the crest; he'd ordered champagne and then they'd enjoyed a meal as delicious as any she could remember. Afterwards, he'd driven her straight back to her hotel with no suggestion of dropping in at his place for a last drink, had said good night in the foyer. During the following days, he'd shown her the island and made everything so interesting because he'd known the history; for instance, in the glass factory, he'd told her how it had been founded by a man who had learned his art in Venice and, braving the threat of execution if he betrayed his artistic knowledge, had come to Mallorca . . .

She'd tried to persuade Mary to join them on many occasions, but without success. She hadn't liked leaving Mary on her own, but wasn't ready to deny herself pleasure just to provide company for someone who was being rather silly . . .

'The relationship stopped being fun on the Saturday, didn't it?' Alvarez said.

'How d'you mean?'

'You must have had a row because Pablo, the gardener, drove you back, not Señor Muir.'

'There wasn't exactly a row . . .'

'Yes?'

'It's embarrassing.'

'Regard me as a priest who can't be embarrassed.'

'It's me who's embarrassed, having to tell you . . . Are you sure you have to know?'

'I'm afraid so.'

She fiddled with the stem of her glass, now almost

empty. She wasn't an innocent abroad. From the beginning, she'd understood that Scott would try to bed her, but with the skill of a good seducer would wine and dine her, make her feel like a princess, before he made his move. When he did, she'd quietly refused his advance. Far from being angered, he'd said he admired her for her old-fashioned standards and apologized for not recognizing the kind of person she really was. Three days later, he had proposed, promising her a golden life . . . She'd said she liked him, very much, but for her, love had to be so much more than liking and it needed time in which to mature. So she hadn't refused him, just set her decision in the future. The next day, he'd suggested a trip in his motor yacht – yet again, Mary had refused to join them. When several miles off the coast, he'd stopped the engines. They'd swum, after which they'd enjoyed a bottle of champagne before the picnic meal, a bottle of wine with that. And he'd become so ardent, it had been very difficult to make him realize she still wouldn't let him make love to her . . .

'It really is terribly embarrassing,' she said. 'It must make you think I . . . I gave him reason to believe . . .'

'I'm quite certain you didn't,' he assured her, with greater certainty than perhaps the facts warranted.

'Men seem to get the wrong idea rather easily.'

'I'm afraid that's so.'

'But when he understood . . . Just like the previous time, he wasn't angry. You really don't think I was to blame?'

'Of course I don't.'

'You're a very sympathetic person, Enrique. It's so wonderful to meet someone like that!' She finished her drink and put the glass down.

Buoyed by her warm praise, he recklessly said: 'Would you like another?'

'I would. It's such a wonderful drink in the heat.'

He signalled to the waitress, who was leaving a nearby table, and she came across. He ordered two more drinks. The waitress left. He offered Tabitha a cigarette, which she refused, lit one. 'Tell me why Señor Muir would not drive you home on the Saturday?'

Muir's behaviour on the motor cruiser, despite his good-natured acceptance of her refusal, had made her hesitant about continuing the relationship, but he possessed the charm of Apollo and she had agreed to go out with him again. He'd taken her to the Casino and provided the money for betting and when she'd been lucky, had refused to take back either the original stake or her winnings; he had dined and wined her at expensive restaurants; and at the end of each evening had asked for no more than a promise to go out again the next day.

On the Friday, he had chartered a private Lear jet to fly them to St-Tropez where they'd dined at the Chabrichon. On their drive back from Palma, he'd suggested calling in at Sa Rotaga. She had not missed his tension and had asked to be taken straight back to the hotel. He had remained pleasant and amusing, but not quite able to hide his angry frustration. However, since he'd made no attempt to challenge her request, she'd judged he was willing, reluctantly, to accept that however golden the life, she was not going to warm his bed unless or until she wanted to. Saturday taught her he had learned nothing. He'd suggested lunch at Sa Rotaga because he had arranged for a special meal . . .

The waitress returned and collected up their empty glasses, put filled ones down on the table. Tabitha sipped her drink and then, after a verbal nudge, continued to tell him what had happened.

Down by the pool, they'd drunk their first glassfuls of Bollinger. Then, very casually, he'd suggested they increase their pleasure. He had had to explain what he meant.

'He was offering you cocaine?'

'How did you know?'

'A guess.'

'Something more than a guess, I think.' She stared out to sea and watched a tyro windsurfer struggling to stay sailing. 'I suppose I shouldn't have been so surprised,' she said finally. 'A lot of people use it.'

'Did you have some?'

Her indignation was immediate. 'You think I'm that stupid? I've a friend, Jill, who went around with a man who was on it and he persuaded her. I tried to tell her, she was risking everything, but she wouldn't listen; swore she'd always be in control. After he dropped her, she lacked easy money for the habit and ended up servicing her pusher even though she loathed him.' She was silent for a moment, then said: 'I told him exactly what I thought of a man who hoped drugs would make a woman more amenable.'

'You thought that was his aim?'

'Is that a serious question?'

'Cocaine is not exactly . . . Never mind. How did he react to your accusation?'

'Swore a bit, laughed a lot, poured more champagne.'

'Yet, despite everything, you stayed to lunch?'

'I don't think you understand the charm of the man. And I suppose it was this charm which persuaded me that he accepted he wasn't going to get what he wanted . . . Hell, how can I explain?'

'You're managing so far.'

'And blackening my character? You're a hard task-master, Enrique, because it's got to be more of a confession than an explanation . . . It's so easy to get used to luxury, so difficult to face losing it. And I was so certain I could control everything and he was such great company when he wasn't trying his darndest to bed me . . .Yes, I stayed to lunch even though I'd lost my appetite, which seemed to annoy that virago of a woman who's his housekeeper. Then after the meal, he said he wanted to show me something . . . Would you believe that in this day and age, a mature woman could be so stupid as to let herself be taken upstairs to see some etchings?'

'That's what he wanted to show you?'

'Of course not. That's just an old joke. He'd bought me a present – a lovely brooch and because I'd drunk rather a lot, I was slow to realize there was a price attached. He became so excited, I had to fight like hell. In the end, I told him to drive me back to my hotel or call a taxi. When he refused, I said if he didn't do something, I'd tell the police he'd damned near tried to rape me.'

'He'd really scared you?'

'Of course he had.'

'Yet when you left Sa Rotaga, you were smiling and Pablo says on the drive back you were cheerful.'

'Has he never heard of trying to hide one's emotions? I wasn't just frightened, I was hating myself. I'd known what kind of a man Scott really was, yet I'd kept hiding the truth from myself. Why? Because he offered a lifestyle I could normally only dream about. I'd almost been seduced, not by him, but his wealth . . . But you can't understand that because you don't believe me.'

'Why do you say that? I believe every word you've told me.'

'Then why try to make out I'm a liar because I was smiling and seemed to be cheerful?'

'There was an apparent inconsistency and so I had to resolve it. You've just made it perfectly clear it was only apparent, not real.'

She drank. 'You . . . you scare me a little, Enrique.'

'You can't think—'

'Not as Scott scared me.'

'Then in what way?'

'I'm not going to explain.'

'That's unfair.'

'Good.'

There was a pause, during which both of them became more aware of the beach sounds around them, before he said: 'Did you learn much about his life?'

'He talked a lot, but seldom about himself. I never even learned how he became so wealthy.'

'Then he never mentioned friends or enemies?'

'I don't think so.'

There seemed to be little more she could tell him. And if they did not move soon, she might well hint at a third daiquiri. 'You'll be glad to hear I don't need to ask you any more embarrassing questions.'

'Very glad.'

'So you can return to be with your friend.'

'I'm in no rush.'

'Sadly, I am.'

After he'd paid the bill, escorted her to where Mary lay, and walked back to his car, he cursed his peasant meanness.

Seventeen

Juan put a spoonful of Arroz al estilo Tossa into his mouth and began to chew. 'Hey!' he said through his mouthful. 'It isn't—' He stopped when Dolores turned to look at him.

'Yes?' she said. Only one word, but there was no missing the ice.

'Nothing,' he mumbled.

'You're being silly,' Isabel jeered.

He tried to kick her under the table, but could not reach.

Jaime began to eat as Dolores served herself. He chewed more and more slowly, looked at Alvarez.

Dolores sat. She spoke to Jaime. 'Is something troubling you?'

He shook his head.

'But you are not eating.' She looked around the table. 'Indeed, no one is eating! Have I spent many hours slaving in the kitchen – as a woman, I was born to sacrifice myself – trying to prepare a tasty meal for my family, only to have them refuse to eat it? Aiyee! Can there be anything more disheartening than to strive to serve, yet be rejected?'

Alvarez reached for the bottle and refilled his glass. In times of trouble, an extra glassful of wine could offer some small comfort.

'Perhaps,' Dolores continued, 'I should not express my feelings. After all, they can be of no account. In this family,

157

as in any other, it is only the men's feelings which need to be considered. And so if the men think the food I have provided is inedible, they must be served something else. There is a little sobrasada which is perhaps not yet so old as to be dangerous. And there is a barra from two days ago which will be stale, but perhaps even stale bread is preferable to a meal prepared by me.'

Alvarez drank and blamed Jaime for not telling his wife to shut up. But Jaime suffered from a cowardly spirit . . .

She faced Alvarez. 'You obviously will prefer sobrasada and bread since you have hardly eaten any of what I have served you.'

'The meal . . . that is . . . the taste is perfect, but . . .'

'Well.'

He drank more wine. 'The rice does not seem to be cooked.'

'You wish to tell me I do not know how to cook rice?'

'No one else can cook it as perfectly as you do. So perhaps there was something wrong with this rice before you cooked it.'

'You are now saying I carelessly did not notice it was bad?'

'Well, it's not exactly right . . .'

'Men have strange ideas about cooking. Possibly, they believe food cooks itself.' She picked up a spoon, filled it from her plate, and ate. After she'd swallowed, she said: 'Indeed, Enrique, you are right, the rice is not cooked. How could such a disaster have occurred?'

'Anyone can get something wrong occasionally,' Jaime said, hoping to soothe her wounded pride.

'And there are those who get everything wrong all the time,' she snapped.

'Perhaps you fell asleep,' Juan suggested.

'It does not occur to you that had I done so, the rice would be overcooked, not undercooked?'

'Stupid!' Isabel jeered.

There was a silence. Dolores ate another mouthful. 'Now I remember!'

They waited.

'There was a phone call from Rosa which so disturbed me that for a while I did not know what I was doing . . . My mother was a very wise woman.'

Jaime silently groaned.

'She often said a man only told the truth when this might prove more useful than a lie.'

They searched their memories, each hoping it was one of the others who had done something to incur her wrath.

'Sharks! Sprats! As I told Rosa, it is not only fishermen who tell fishy stories.'

Alvarez remembered these were his words of the morning, but could not understand why they were returning to haunt him.

'And as Rosa said to me, age does not matter. An old man is as ready to make a fool of himself as a young man . . . Juana, Isabel, you will leave the table.'

'But we haven't eaten,' Isabel said uneasily.

'What I have to say is not for your ears. When you return, I may have managed to produce a meal which people will deign to eat.'

They hurried out of the room.

'Who,' Dolores said with considerable intensity, 'could believe my cousin would lie to me and say he had to get to work early when in truth it was his intention to sit on the beach and drink with a naked woman?'

'Do what?' said Jaime.

'She wasn't naked . . .' Alvarez began.

'I think I have too generous a nature. I still try to tell

159

myself, perhaps you lied not primarily to deceive me, but to save me the shocked embarrassment of knowing you intended to sit in public with a naked woman.'

'She was wearing—'

'Rosa mentioned she was young.' Dolores stood. 'Of course she was young, since no older woman could lack all sense of propriety. As I said to Rosa, I had to confess, however much it pained me to do so, that my cousin searches ever more desperately for youth as he grows older.' She paused, looked round the table; no one met her gaze. 'I might cook the meal a little longer so that the rice is all right, but then perhaps it will not taste as it should. But that will not concern you two men since by then you will have drunk too much to taste anything.' She reached out to pick up each plate in turn and empty it into the cooking pot, carried that through to the kitchen.

Jaime drank deeply. He leaned forward and spoke quietly, but excitedly. 'She really was starkers?'

'Don't be so bloody stupid.'

'But there are nude beaches.'

'Port Llueso isn't one of them and even if it were, do you think I'd be bothered to visit it?'

'If you had the chance.'

'She was wearing a bikini.'

'Must have been almost invisible for Rosa to say she was naked.'

'Women always magnify or diminish things.'

Jaime thought about that. 'All the same, she was obviously something for Rosa to be bothered to ring Dolores.'

'She is something.'

'And you're taking her out tonight?'

'I only got in touch because she's a witness and, just possibly, a potential suspect.'

'Whatever, you might have chatted her up when she was dressed so we didn't have to suffer a ruined meal.'

Alvarez refilled his glass.

He parked in front of Sa Rotaga, opened the front door, entered the hall and called out. Elena, wearing an apron and holding a dust mop in her right hand, came through an inner doorway. 'Still hard at work, then,' he said.

'You expect otherwise?'

He sighed. Women could be so very difficult. 'That was meant as a compliment.'

'It would be better if you kept your compliments to yourself.'

'I've dropped in to have a quick word.'

'Then you can say it in the kitchen since me and Pablo are having a short break.'

'For which you've cooked something?'

'Coques de les Monges. I suppose you'll want some?'

'So long as that doesn't deprive anyone.'

'As if you'd worry if it did!'

He followed her into the kitchen. Ortiz, seated at the table, greeted him, then said to Elena: 'The coffee's just made.'

As she crossed to the stove, she said: 'Of course, it didn't occur to you to get on your feet and turn off the gas.'

Home from home, Alvarez thought, as he sat.

The cake/sponge was as soft as an angel's sigh and he told her so. It was clear she viewed his praise as no more than her due.

'What are you after now?' she asked, as she stirred her mug of coffee.

'To learn how things were on the Saturday.'

'The same as most days.'

'Which means him hard after a woman,' Ortiz said.

'Enough!' she snapped.

161

Ortiz spoke to Alvarez. 'With him dead, she don't like to hear things as they really were.'

'Will you wish people to blacken you when you're dead?' she asked.

'Can't see how it'll worry me.' He grinned. 'Not so long as I've had all the pleasure when I was alive.'

Alvarez said: 'I had a talk with Tabitha this morning and asked how things had been with Señor Muir.'

'Must have been interesting!' Ortiz remarked.

'Surprising. She says she resisted him all the way.'

'Well, I don't know I'd be that ready to call her a liar.' Ortiz leaned forward and cut himself another slice of Coques.

'Why's that?'

'Because I wondered more'n once what sort of luck he was having.'

'No you didn't, not from how you was always talking,' she said.

He ignored her. 'It was the way he looked at her, kind of surprised and angry . . . Didn't you notice?' he asked Elena.

'I do not waste my time, ever.'

'Haven't I heard you say more than once in the past that he was in a good temper because he'd enjoyed picking the cherry and there was one more fool of a woman in the world?'

'Would I make such a ridiculous comment?'

Alvarez ate the last piece of Coques on his plate. 'When I spoke to you before, you said Tabitha and Señor Muir had a row that Saturday.'

They looked at each other to decide who should answer.

'Did either of you actually hear them rowing?'

'Can't say I did,' she answered.

'Me, neither,' Ortiz said.

'Then you were basing your judgement on the fact the señor asked you to drive her down to the port instead of doing that himself?'

'And the way he told me to do it; and how they were with each other,' Ortiz answered.

'How did they behave to each other?'

Ortiz was about to answer, but Elena spoke first. 'Why are you asking all these questions about her?'

'To find out what was their relationship.'

'What's it matter now he's dead?'

'The law needs to know.'

'The law!' she said with the contempt all Mallorquins had for that.

'Were they on friendly terms during the meal?'

'The meal I took such care to cook and she disliked so much she ate almost nothing? How can I tell how they were?'

Ortiz said: 'You told me they were being more than friendly when you went into the dining room unexpectedly . . .'

'I told you nothing.'

'After the meal, they went upstairs?' said Alvarez.

Her expression of disapproval was her answer.

'When they returned downstairs, how were they?'

'He was in a temper and as rude as only an unthinking foreigner can be; do they think they buy us when they pay us wages?'

'And how was she?'

'Acting like the puta she is.'

'What does that mean?'

'You wish me to believe you don't know how a puta behaves? . . . She was all false smiles.'

Alvarez turned to Ortiz. 'When you drove down to her hotel, did she say much?'

'She can't speak Spanish.'

'She was silent?'

'She spoke a little, only I couldn't understand.'

'But didn't you tell me before, she was so cheerful you wondered—?'

'What she was thinking,' Ortiz said hastily, before his actual words could be repeated.

'I wonder how Águenda would like to know her husband is interested in a puta's thoughts?' Elena said sarcastically.

'I wasn't thinking what you think I was.'

Alvarez hastily changed the conversation before a row developed between the other two. 'Your coques is so delicious, could I possibly have another small slice? And perhaps another cup of coffee?'

'Are men's appetites ever satisfied?' she wondered aloud as she cut a large slice.

Alvarez turned off the main road and drove along the narrow, twisting lane until he reached Ortiz's finca. A typical small farmhouse – originally the human accommodation had been on the top floor, the animal accommodation on the bottom one – it and a couple of small outbuildings were in a two-hectare field.

'Pablo is not here,' Águenda said, after he had introduced himself.

'That's all right, it's you I want to talk to.' She was thin, her facial skin had been leathered by work in the fields and her features were as sharp as her manner; he was certain that she would be censoriously interested in her husband's interest in a puta's thoughts.

'Why should you want to talk to me?'

'Just to ask you where Pablo was on a Saturday afternoon.'

'What Saturday?'

Had she been of a more welcoming nature, she would have asked him into the sitting-room, suggested he sat, and observed that no doubt he would welcome a coffee; as it was, clearly he was going to be left standing just inside the entrada. 'The Saturday he had to work at Sa Rotaga in the afternoon, the Saturday of the weekend when the señor died.'

'Well?'

Small wonder that Ortiz had amused himself looking through the hedge at Muir's amatory pleasures; a man had to find some enjoyment in life. 'He drove Elena to her home; did he then return here?'

'Of course.'

'So he arrived here at about what time?'

'You do not know how long it takes to drive to Llueso and then to here?'

'Yes, of course, but—'

'So why ask?'

'I have to be certain he did drive straight from the village to here.'

'You think he would do otherwise?'

It seemed very doubtful. 'Can you tell me roughly when he arrived here?'

'I do not watch the clock as some people do.' She was staring at him as she said that.

'But you're satisfied he did come straight here after dropping Elena at her home?'

'Why should I be satisfied?'

He sighed. 'You are convinced that's what he did?'

'Naturally.'

'Was he here for the rest of the evening?'

'You think he would spend time in a bar when there is so much work to do?'

Running along the side of the house he had noticed rows

of peas, beans, tomatoes, peppers, lettuces, aubergines, onions, and garlic, growing strongly thanks to plenty of water; in front of the house were olive, fig, orange, lemon, and almond trees; from one of the outhouses had come the sounds of pigs. It was doubtful either of them had any spare time. They were a family who still believed it necessary to do everything possible to be self-sufficient because disaster was always waiting. 'And was he here all night?'

'You ask stupid questions,' she said, adding a Mallorquin adjective that was seldom used except by country people who were very earthy.

He assumed that she was agreeing Ortiz had spent the night in her company. He thanked her for her help and left, certain her beady eyes would suspiciously watch him until he had driven out of sight.

The phone rang as Alvarez was about to leave the office. Inclination was to ignore the call, but to do so might give the impression he had stopped work rather early.

Traffic told him they were trying to fax a list of cars, but were unable to do so because of a problem at his end; would he correct the fault? He went downstairs to the room in which the fax machine was kept, convinced he would achieve nothing because he was not of the digital age. For once, his pessimism was unwarranted. The fault was lack of paper. He brought a new roll out of a drawer, inserted it, decided he'd got it the wrong way round and reversed it.

He telephoned Traffic in Palma and said to fax him again.

The list of Jaguars recently bought was larger than he'd expected and confirmed yet again how prosperous was the island. The fifth name was Valeriano Yague.

He returned to his office, climbing the stairs slowly,

and slumped down in his chair, all thoughts of an early departure from the office temporarily forgotten.

If he took no further action, he should be safe; if he continued with his forbidden investigation, took the next and possibly conclusive step, there had to be the strong possibility his actions would be exposed and the consequences of that had been made all too clear by Salas. But how could he stop now, when proof of his suspicions might be only a phone call away, how could he turn his back on the chance to save the Wilderness?

The directory provided the phone number of the Jaguar distributors. He spoke to an assistant manger, who listened to his request, then said. 'You do mean, the minister?'

'Yes.'

'And you want to know how he paid for his car?'

'That's right.'

'I'm not certain . . . You know, things can be tricky when a politician's concerned. I suppose you have the authority for asking for this information?'

'As I told you, I am an inspector in the Cuerpo . . .'

'No offence, but in the circumstances it really needs the authority of someone of higher rank.'

'Would my superior chief suffice or should I call on the director-general?'

'Your superior chief will get in touch with us and confirm?'

'I don't know how he'll react to being asked to do that since it's he who ordered me to ask you for the information.'

'Then you can quote his authority for this request?'

'I don't see why not.'

'I'll accept that. Shall I ring you back when I have the answer?'

'If you would.'

'I suppose . . . You wouldn't like to say what it's about, would you?'

'Sorry, but as you pointed out earlier, when a politician is involved, one keeps one's head well down.'

When he replaced the receiver, Alvarez thought he might just have thrown his career into the dustbin. He tried to recall what had motivated him into taking so great a risk? Had he really seen the fate of the Wilderness as more important than his own? . . . His fears grew to such an extent that when the phone rang, he was convinced the caller was Salas, informing him he was now ex-inspector . . .

The assistant manager told him that payment had been slightly unusual since it had been in cash.

He stared unseeingly through the window. Using Vives as the go-between, Muir had bribed Yague to approve the development of the Wilderness; the first tranche of money had been paid earlier in the year, the second would have been paid once Muir had gained the land with planning permission. Politicians were forever surviving the suspicion they were crooked, but never the proof of this. How to prove that the cash which paid for the Jaguar had come from Muir?

He would have been surprised to have been reminded that only minutes before he had come to the conclusion he would have to be of a suicidal nature to pursue the investigation any further.

Eighteen

On Thursday morning, Alvarez arrived early at the post, to the expressed amazement of the duty cabo, who put down the girlie magazine he had been reading. 'I'm seeing, but I can't believe!'

Alvarez ignored the stupidity and continued up to his office, where he settled in his chair after switching on the fan to maximum power. How to prove bribery? . . . Muir had drawn the money in cash. If all from one bank and in one draft, that bank would have had to be advised beforehand. Would it have recorded the number of the notes, would these all have been in sequence; would anyone at the garage have noted the numbers of at least some of those paid? Was anything more un-likely?

The phone rang.

Salas spoke with increasing anger. 'I have been in command of the Cuerpo on this island for more years than I care to remember. During this time, I have occasionally and regrettably had to deal with the subordinate who has proved himself to be ignorant, generally incompetent, perhaps even totally incapable, but until now I have never had to suffer one individual in whom all those undesirable qualities are combined.'

There was a silence.

'Have you nothing to say?'

169

'Señor, I am not quite certain what I am expected to say.'

'The offer of your resignation would be welcome.'

'But . . . I don't understand.'

'Did I order you not to pursue enquiries concerning the ridiculous accusations you saw fit to make?'

'You are referring to the possible bribery of—'

'You will not mention a name.'

'The fact is—'

'The fact is, you suffer an inability to be able to distinguish fact from fiction.'

'But the evidence concerning Vives suggests there has been bribery; the possibility of the development of the Wilderness suggests a target for that bribery; the initials on two of the bundles of notes in Señor Muir's safe suggest—'

'For a suggestion to be considered seriously, it has to possess at least some gleaning of intelligence.'

'The minister—'

'Refrain from mentioning rank.'

'The person in question recently bought a Jaguar. Do you know how much that costs?'

'Of course I do not.'

'Perhaps a hundred thousand euros. This sum was paid in cash. Who has even a tithe of that much in cash unless it is black? Assume it was black and—'

'You will make no such assumption. As I said to the person to whom I was speaking when he phoned me this morning . . . Understandably, he was almost incoherent with rage.'

Ministers, Alvarez thought, usually were incoherent, since then they could not be understood.

'A man in his position, of spotless character, having his integrity questioned by a mere inspector! . . . I explained how, most regrettably, you had been allowed to join the force before the standards of entry had become reasonably high. Initially, that failed to pacify him as he seemed to believe originally I had ordered the investigation into matters which concerned him and it took me a considerable time to explain that the moment I learned of your ridiculous inquiries, I ordered you to drop them. He then, understandably, if inaccurately, pointed out that since you clearly had not obeyed my orders, there must be a lack of authority on my part . . . Goddamnit, why should I suffer for your incompetent stupidity?'

'Señor, surely the . . . the person in question should explain how he came into possession of so large a sum in cash?'

'Why?'

'To counter the presumption—'

'There can be no presumption.'

'Normally, no one would deal in so large a sum in cash; such a payment would be made by cheque—'

'As the person to whom I was talking was at pains to point out, he cannot possibly be under any obligation to explain anything. However, being as he described himself, a man who values honesty above rubies, he insisted on explaining the facts, despite my expressed embarrassment at listening to them. His cousin, an unmarried man – whose cooking, he said, proved conclusively he was in no way related to the very famous chef; despite his anger, he allowed his sense of humour to shine through – lived near Perpignan. Sadly, his cousin was elderly and as can happen, his wits dimmed and he developed the fear he was in danger of becoming penniless; as a consequence, he lived like a miser, even though his income was considerable. The money saved was kept in cash in various hiding places about his house. When he died recently, hundreds of thousands of euros were found, together with many francs which he had not, for some reason, changed. Being his sole heir, the person in question travelled to Perpignan to sort out the estate and arrange for the sale of the property – which has not yet occurred. Faced with handling this large amount in cash, knowing banks never miss a chance to levy iniquitous fees for doing the slightest service, he decided to carry it back to this island. As he admitted – he is not too grand a man to lack humility – it was a silly thing to do. The saving would be relatively small, the suitcases might be stolen, the plane might crash, customs might demand, despite his rank, he open the suitcases and not immediately understand the circumstances . . . However, fortune was with him. Twice over, as he was amused to say. Once home, knowing he intended to buy a new car, he did not bank the money; so, when he collected the car, he paid for it in cash . . . What do you have to say now?'

'He has a wonderful imagination.'

'Is there no limit to your stupid insolence?' Salas shouted.

'If you ask me, which you did, Señor, he unexpectedly found he had to come up with an explanation and possessing far more imagination than ability—'

'Silence!'

There was silence.

'You will apologize for daring to suggest the person in question is a liar.'

'You want me to phone him—'

'Talking to you, Alvarez, demands more patience than any saint ever possessed. It is impossible to conceive anything I wish less than that you should speak a single word to him; God knows what chaos would ensue.'

'Then who am I to apologize to?'

'Who the devil do you think? To me.'

'But where's the point in apologizing to you for something which concerns him?'

Salas slammed down the receiver.

Alvarez poured himself a drink, gloomily noting as he did so that the bottle was almost empty. He had pursued his investigation into the money in Muir's safe because he had believed the Wilderness was threatened. Since his only motive had been to save a little of the past for the present and the future, it surely was an objective to be praised. Yet the superior chief had been quite unable to understand . . . He finished the drink, looked at the bottle, emptied it into the glass. It was, he decided, he who couldn't understand; understand he was a fool to believe one totally unimportant person could alter anything. How could he have imagined that any action of his would ever be of the slightest consequence; how could he have forgotten that the gods of profit were all-powerful?

The phone rang.

'The superior chief wants to know why he has not received a report on the evidence the Marshes have given?' the plum-voiced secretary said.

'Whose evidence?'

'Marshes.'

'I'm afraid that for the moment I don't recognize the name.'

'Wait.'

He heard voices, but could not make out the words spoken. Then Salas said: 'My secretary confesses she has great difficulty in understanding you. I have informed her that that fact is a compliment to her intelligence. Why have I not received a report on your questioning of the Marshes?'

'I'm afraid I can't place the name, Señor.'

173

'Should I be surprised? Perhaps not. Incompetence knows no boundaries. According to you, Locke's evidence is in flat contradiction to that of the servants at Sa Rotaga.'

'Now I remember . . . I'm sorry, Señor, but there have been so many difficult and complicated problems to deal with . . .'

'Most of which should not have begun to concern you. Do the Marshes corroborate Locke's statement or the servants'?'

'I'm not quite certain.'

'Their evidence is ambiguous?'

'In a way.'

'In what way?'

'I think it will be best if I have another word with them . . .'

'Your evasiveness suggests the depths of your inefficiency have still to be plumbed. Have you yet questioned them?'

'Señor, I have been so busy . . .'

'So busy pursuing a ridiculous figment of your imagination, so eager to slander another's reputation, you have ignored the case you are supposedly investigating. Your ineptitude places you on a plane of your own.'

'But I—'

'Were it possible, I should replace you immediately; since it is not, you will question the Marshes and report to me the moment you have done so.' Salas rang off.

It was not his day . . . And he was an even bigger fool than had been suggested. He had forgotten to explain he had not questioned the Marshes because he was waiting for information from the English police . . .

He finished his drink and reached for the bottle, found it was empty.

Nineteen

Ca'n Bastoyne was built in Ibicencan style, its flat roofs distinguishing it from all other bungalows in the urbanizacíon. Thirteen steps had to be climbed to reach the small porch and Alvarez arrived there sweating and short of breath.

The door was opened by a middle-aged woman he knew. Raquel had an officious manner and an over-developed interest in other people's faults, but she was an acquaintance of Dolores so he assured her it was an unexpected pleasure to meet her and how were her family? Having, hopefully, ensured she would not complain about him to Dolores, he asked if the Marshes were at home.

'They're out by the pool.'

As she led the way through the sitting room, she complained strongly about the Marshes and their foreign habits; he assumed she was certain that they, like most foreigners, spoke no Mallorquin.

To the right of the house, where the slope of the land was least, was an oblong swimming pool, its length three times that of its width. By the shallow end, was set a large sun umbrella and under its shade a man sat at a bamboo and glass table. A woman in a full bathing costume lay on a lilo in the pool.

Alvarez introduced himself.

'You're the chappy asking questions because of Scott's death?' Marsh asked.

'That is so, Señor.'

'Nasty affair; very nasty. I suppose you'd like a chat with us? Naturally, if we can be of any help, we will be.'

An offer, Alvarez noted, made uneasily.

'Do sit. And you'll have a drink?'

'Thank you. Perhaps I might have a coñac with just ice.'

'It's Liberty Hall, so provided it's not a bottle of Tokay, you can have what you want.' He laughed nervously before he turned to Raquel and in halting, just decipherable Spanish, asked her to bring a brandy for the inspector and another gin and tonic for himself.

As Raquel returned to the house, there was a call from the pool. 'Who is it, Neville?'

'The police.'

'What does he want?'

'I don't yet know.'

As she began to paddle the lilo towards the steps, Alvarez said, 'Did you know Señor Muir had been stabbed?'

Marsh's shocked surprise was obvious. 'We heard he'd died from drowning. And that's what the papers said.'

'That was the cause of death, but the reason he fell into the swimming pool and lacked the strength, and perhaps also the will, to save himself was because he had bled so severely after being stabbed.'

'Good God!'

Evelyn slid off the lilo, climbed the steps and came around the pool. As soon as she was near, Marsh said: 'Scott was stabbed before he drowned.'

She came to a stop. As the water dripped off her, she stared at her husband for several seconds, her expression worried. 'Then . . . it wasn't an accident?'

'No.'

She walked forward and Marsh introduced her. She

176

moved one of the patio chairs out of the shade of the umbrella into the sunshine, sat. 'I imagine you're here to ask if we can help in any way? Frankly, he was not – how shall I put it? – he was not the kind of person with whom we had much in common. We were invited to his parties and naturally returned hospitality, but we didn't meet frequently. In fact, we'd no idea he was married until we heard that through local gossip.'

Marsh said: 'We weren't alone in that. I don't think anyone even guessed. After all, when one sees a man enjoying the company of a succession of very snazzy women, one tends to think he's footloose and fancy free.'

'Or has a wife of very small intelligence,' she said.

She had a friendly manner but, Alvarez judged, there was a measure of steel behind the friendliness. And as were so many women, she was jealous of a man's pleasures. 'As a matter of fact, although I should like to know anything relevant you can tell me concerning Señor Muir, I am not here primarily to ask you about him.'

'Why are you here, then?' she asked.

Before Alvarez could answer, Raquel came out of the house and crossed to the table, put two glasses down on it. Evelyn said: 'Would you bring me a Cinzano with some ice and a slice of lemon, please?' Her Spanish was far better than her husband's, a common trait amongst foreign couples who lived on the island.

As Raquel returned to the house, Evelyn said to Alvarez: 'Are you telling us that Scott was murdered?'

'He died because he was stabbed, Señora.'

'It couldn't have been an accident?'

'I have searched and found nothing which, had he fallen on to it, might have caused the injuries.'

'I only asked because . . . it seems so impossible anyone would deliberately kill him.'

'It is always difficult to accept violence, Señora.' But was that what was so clearly worrying her or was it the fact she could guess her husband and she were going to be asked to verify Locke's alibi? And while it had seemed there could be no great harm in doing that if Muir had accidentally drowned, it became a very different matter if he had been deliberately attacked.

Raquel returned, handed Evelyn a glass, left.

Evelyn said, trying to change the conversation: 'It must have been very difficult living in this heat before refrigerators were invented.'

'For the poor, it was; for the wealthy, there was the ice from the mountains which had been stored . . . Señora, I understand you and the señor are friends of Señor and Señora Locke?'

She looked quickly at her husband, her expression tight; he met her gaze for a moment, then looked away. 'That's right.'

'They have told you I asked them many questions?'

'They said something, but I can't remember what.'

'Then it will be best if I explain. There is evidence that someone drove up to Sa Rotaga a little after five on the afternoon on the Saturday on which Señor Muir died. Obviously, I should very much like to speak to the driver of that car and—'

'Are you suggesting it was he who killed Scott?' Marsh asked, his voice high.

'I am suggesting nothing because I do not know who he was or why he was going to the house . . . Señor, how did you know the driver of the car was a man?'

'What do you mean?'

Evelyn said quickly: 'My husband is old enough to be sufficiently biased to think few women can drive, so he regards all drivers as male. A Pavlovian reaction.'

Marsh drank.

'The señor employed two staff, Elena and Pablo . . .'

'We know them,' Marsh said hurriedly. 'Charming people.'

'They were working there that Saturday. As they were about to drive away in Pablo's car to return to their homes, the señor came out of the house – his guest had left earlier and he was on his own – and when asked if he wanted something, shook his head. Since he made no mention of being injured, did not request their help which an injured man would have done, we can be sure that when they left, he was uninjured. On their drive towards the public road, they passed a car going to Sa Rotaga. They told me that Señor Locke was driving it.'

'Impossible,' she said.

'Elena has no doubts, Pablo is perhaps not certain.'

'They're both wrong.'

'Why do you say that?'

'Laura and Keir were here at that time, as they must have told you. You're trying to make out they're liars, aren't you?'

'Steady on,' Marsh said.

'We are not going to be called liars,' she said fiercely.

'Señora,' Alvarez said, 'please understand I am not suggesting you are a liar. My problem is, I am faced by a conflict of evidence and I have to try to resolve this.'

'Of course we understand,' Marsh said.

Alvarez noticed her brief expression of annoyance at her husband's intervention.

'I'm sorry if I sounded rude,' she said, 'but if you think the servants were right, then you have to believe us to be wrong and therefore lying when we tell you Laura and Keir were here. The fact is, they were here.'

'Is there any way in which you could corroborate that, Señora?'

'Our word is not good enough?'

'For me, of course, but I have a superior chief who would demand to examine the halo before he would accept that the person wearing it was a saint.'

'Very well. I keep a diary, so I'll go inside and check the entry for that Saturday and make certain it confirms my memory. Then you'll be able to assure your Doubting Thomas that the two servants had to be mistaken.'

Marsh cleared his throat, as if about to speak. She looked at him and he remained silent.

'Señora, I shall be glad when I can be certain. However, I do think it would be best if you show me the entry in your diary so that I can tell my superior I have read it.'

'My dear inspector, don't you understand a woman keeps a diary in part to remember her secrets? No, you may not read what I've written because I may have included something which even my husband is not allowed to know. But I can assure you I will tell you everything but my secrets. Isn't that good enough?'

'For me, of course. But my superior chief—'

'Will have to learn to judge a halo by instinct.' She stood, her costume now so dry that she scattered no drops of water as she moved, crossed the pool patio to the house.

Marsh drank. 'Women can be funny,' he said uneasily.

'Indeed.'

'Very secretive about some things.'

'There was a Mallorquin philosopher who wrote that it is secrecy, not truth, which makes for a happy marriage.'

'I'd guess his wife didn't know the half of what went on . . . Will you have another drink?'

'Thank you.'

'I'll get it rather than bother Raquel again.'

As Marsh left, Alvarez stared out at the small segment of the bay which was visible to the right of a wild olive tree. Truth always had the ability to be dangerous, within or without a marriage.

Evelyn and Marsh returned together; he passed a glass to Alvarez, put another down on the table, sat. He drank with nervous eagerness.

'There were no secrets that day,' she said, 'so I can quote verbatim. L and K – Laura and Keir – arrived unannounced to interrupt our siesta with a chocolate praline sponge bought in the port. Delicious, but very bad for the scales . . . I did wonder whether to withhold that comment since it reveals a worry about weight . . . L and K very cheerful. Arranged to go into Palma together to the concert at the Auditorium.'

'And you wrote that on Saturday, the thirteenth of this month?'

'I did. Just before going to bed.'

'Did you note the time of their arrival?'

'No, but I can tell you reasonably accurately. Keir is still slave to a few puritanical standards, not having lived here long enough to shed them all, and refuses most times to enjoy a siesta. As I told him that afternoon when he woke us up, it's the vandals who don't do as the Romans do. When the front door rang and there were no signs of Neville's surfacing, I had to put on a dressing-gown and go to the front door. Keir said he and Laura had come to tea. When I told him it was a criminal offence to call on anyone before five in the afternoon, he laughed, said it was near enough to five to be perfectly legal and quoted . . . What was it he said?' She asked her husband.

'I was asleep.'

'Of course you were,' she agreed hurriedly. 'It was from that breathless poem about filling unforgiving minutes.

I could have hit him for being so pedantically cheer-ful.'

'But you didn't note the time down in your diary?'

'It simply wasn't of any importance. It was being awoken that was.'

'How long did they stay here?'

'I can't give you an exact figure.'

'A rough one would help.'

'I suppose they left around ten, since they stopped for supper. Wouldn't you agree, ten?' She asked her husband.

'About then,' Marsh muttered.

Alvarez thought for a moment, said: 'Thank you for your help. I hope I haven't disturbed you too much?'

'No disturbance. And that's all you want to know?'

'Yes, thank you.'

Minutes later, as Alvarez began to drive slowly down the sloping road – a locked brake, a blow-out, broken steering, and the car could be over the edge – he wondered whether she even kept a diary.

He was half-way to Llueso when he suddenly braked to a halt, to the annoyance of the driver of the car behind who, as he swung out and passed, raised his upright middle finger to express his opinion of Alvarez's standard of driving. It was a wasted gesture. Alvarez stared unseeingly through the windscreen as he gloomily judged Salas might ring and demand confirmation he had checked the alibis of Jemima Muir and Grant and therefore it was now necessary to do just that.

There was a bar in the direct line of sight of Club Gusto and Alvarez went inside, ordered a coñac, and spoke to the barman after identifying himself.

'You're asking me to remember two people who might have been here when we have hundreds in every day?'

182

Hundreds had to be a gross exaggeration. The bar was small, without a pleasing ambience, and set back from the tourist beaches and shopping areas; thirsty patrons of Club Gusto would do their drinking in the club. 'They were English and she was quite a bit older than he. She was kind of shopworn and he was a bit of a loud mouth . . .' He went on to describe Jemima and Grant as sharply as possible.

'It's a long time ago,' said the barman.

'Not all that long, surely.'

'We get a lot of foreigners.'

Few of whom would ever return. 'But there won't be many couples where the woman's trailing a toy boy.'

'Maybe not.'

'Suppose you pour me another drink and give yourself one while you think about things.'

His generosity paid dividends. The barman remembered a foreigner who'd argued about the change he'd been given. 'Anyone can make a mistake,' he remarked with virtuous annoyance. 'His woman was old enough to be his mother.'

How Jemima would appreciate that comment! Alvarez thought. 'Were they English?'

'Sounded like it.'

'When was this?'

'Couldn't rightly say.'

'Have a guess.'

'A week; a couple of weeks.'

'What day was it?'

'How the hell would I remember that?'

'How long were they here?'

'Long enough for him to get half cut.'

'Were they here for as much as an hour, would you think?'

'Longer. Then they went off for a hamburger, or something, before they came back.'

'How long were they away?'

The barman shrugged his shoulders.

'When did they finally leave?'

'When it opened.' He indicated the Club Gusto, just visible through the window. 'From the look of her, she wouldn't have enjoyed the show.'

'You're right, she didn't. Did you chance to hear either of their names?'

'You think I've nothing better to do than listen to people?'

The barman's evidence was too vague to be in any way positively corroborative of Jemima's and Grant's evidence, yet in a negative sense it was. How many English couples, where the wife was so noticeably older than her companion and the man was naturally aggressive, would in the relatively recent past have spent a considerable time in this bar as they waited for the Club Gusto to open? For Alvarez, here was the proof that they had been in the bar for a considerable time from early evening before they went across to the club. But which evening?

He finished his drink and left the bar. Club Gusto – a square building with high roof and not a single pleasing feature – looked dowdily uninteresting from the outside. Its motto could have been, 'Never judge the contents from the cover'. Throughout the island, Club Gusto was recognized as presenting the raunchiest of floor shows. One of the side doors was open and he entered. He spoke to one of the cleaning women who directed him to an office at the far end. Salinas, middle aged, features seemingly slightly askew, greeted him with a handshake. He listened, then said: 'I doubt I can help. For weeks, I've had to replace a chap who was involved in a nasty car crash and run things during the day, making certain everything's ready for the evening.'

'When do you leave in the evening?'

'If nothing's gone wrong, I clear off as soon as I hand over after we open; if something's gone wrong, I can be here half the night.'

It was small wonder the other's face was so pale, he might have lived in northern Europe. 'Who relieves you?'

'Alfonso. He's here until we close.'

'Would he keep a watch on customers who might make a nuisance of themselves?'

'Only in general terms. If there's trouble brewing and it looks like diplomacy won't work, he'll leave it to the security staff to quieten things down.'

'So they're more likely to remember the couple I'm interested in?'

'It's possible. When are we talking about?'

'Twelve nights ago.'

'Twelve nights is a long time in this business.'

'Nevertheless, I'd like a word with someone from the security staff.'

'Best speak to Martine Ques, who's not nearly as dumb as he looks.'

'Where will I find him?'

'In bed, like as not.'

Fifteen minutes later, Alvarez parked in front of a six-storey block of flats, built some years before, which lay well back from the sea. A lift took him up to the third floor and flat 3c; a woman, young, heavily made-up, dressed in a tight-fitting blouse and skirt, opened the door. He guessed she worked at the club. In answer to his question, she said Ques was in bed, but awake.' Will you tell him I want to talk to him.'

She hesitated.

'He's not in any trouble,' he assured her.

'Didn't think he was,' she lied unconvincingly. 'You'd best come in, then.'

The sitting/dining room was long and thin and beyond was a small balcony. He sat on the settee, new and cheap. There were no curtains over the French windows and the small carpet was stained in one corner. On two of the walls hung framed prints of chocolate-box quality, on one of the shelves of an otherwise empty bookcase were stacked a number of tapes and discs; beyond this was a large flat television and a music centre; on the dining table were dirty plates, glasses, a half-empty bottle of wine, and an earthenware bowl in which were several apples. Not a home, a flat in which two people lived.

Five minutes later, Ques, built along battleship lines, best described as powerfully ugly, dressed in dirty T-shirt and shorts, came into the room. 'You're wanting something?' He slumped down on one of the two easy chairs.

'To ask you to help me.'

'Like how?' He turned to shout at the open doorway: 'Where's the coffee?'

'I'm getting it,' was the answer.

He fiddled with a spot on the side of his chin as Alvarez explained what he wanted to know. 'That's too long ago to remember anything.'

'One or two things should have marked them out. For a start, she was noticeably older than him.'

'Don't get that many women,' he observed.

Hardly surprising. 'They came into the club as soon as it opened and didn't leave until late – maybe not until it closed. He was drinking heavily and it's my guess that when he's had a tankful, he causes trouble.'

The woman came into the room and spoke to Alvarez. 'Want some coffee?'

'No, thanks.'

She turned and left.

Ques reached over to a low table, picked up a pack of cigarettes and tapped one out, lit it. After a while, he said: 'Some time back there was a drunken slob tried to climb up on to the stage and join in the act – had to kick him back to his seat. He'd a woman, older than him, who wasn't amused, not by a bloody long shot. They was English.'

'When was this?'

'Can't rightly say.'

'Describe them.'

Since it was always difficult for an untrained person to describe someone in meaningful terms, Alvarez had not expected any description to be of much use; to his surprise, he was given word pictures which left him in little doubt these were describing Jemima and Grant.

'How long were they here?'

'All the time we was open. He must have near drunk us dry on his own.'

'When did you close that night?'

'Can't say. Could've been four or five. Mostly we don't shut while there's enough people drinking. 'Course, the last show's at three. The boys can't keep going all night.'

'What state was he in when they left?'

'Legless.'

'Can you fix which day of the week this was?'

'Didn't I say?'

'You did, but try harder.'

The woman came into the room, carrying a tray which she put on the low table after pushing the pack of cigarettes to one side. 'I've put the sugar in.' She turned to Alvarez. 'There's some biscuits.'

He thanked her, helped himself to a chocolate digestive.

'He wants to know about something what happened at the club,' Ques said, as he stirred the coffee.

She sat.

'Thinks I'm a bloody memory man. When was they here?' Ques drank, careless of the noise he made. 'I remember 'em, but that's all.'

'Who are they?' she asked.

Alvarez was about to answer, when Ques cut in. 'He thought he'd get up on the stage with the girls and show 'em how it's really done. Me and Francisco sorted him out. His woman seemed to think we was killing the silly bastard and screamed blue murder until we persuaded her to shut up.'

'Was she the one you tried to get off with?'

'Belt up.'

'Saw you chatting her up. Thought it would be all right when he was a goner, didn't you?'

'You didn't see nothing.'

She spoke to Alvarez while she stared at Ques. 'Cook his meals, buy his booze, pay the rent, and he says thank you by running after other women.'

'Never laid hands on any of the girls,' Ques said angrily.

'Not because you haven't tried. Not got the right money to interest 'em, have you?'

'Can you tell me when this couple were at the club?' Alvarez asked her.

'Only that it was a Saturday.'

'You sound very certain?'

'Wasn't working the next day 'cause it was a Sunday.'

'How many Saturdays back was it?'

'How d'you mean?'

'Was it last Saturday, the one before that, or when?'

She thought. 'It was the day before I saw my sister what

wasn't last Sunday because that's when she went over to
Menorca to see our dad.'

'When did you see your sister?'

'The Sunday before.'

'It's Saturday, two weeks ago, when this couple were in
the club and you were worried Martine might be—'

'Might be? He was trying his hardest because her man
was too drunk to notice. He'd have given the punters
another show if she'd been willing.'

'I wasn't interested,' Ques shouted.

'You'd a funny way of showing that!'

'How certain can you both be that the English couple
we're talking about were in the club two Saturdays ago?'
Alvarez asked.

'Don't we keep saying?' Ques demanded angrily.

'I'm near enough sure,' she said.

A pedant might have claimed that near enough was not
near enough, but Alvarez was satisfied Jemima and Grant
had been in the bar and then Club Gusto throughout the
late afternoon and until four or five the next morning.

Alvarez rested his feet on the desk and considered his visit
to the Marshes. Marsh had been very nervous. Because
he was naturally of a nervous nature? Evelyn had done
most of the talking. Because she knew her husband to be
a poor liar?

Adela's evidence – if gossip could be called evidence –
had suggested Locke might have had a very strong motive
for assaulting Muir. In which case, it had to be very likely
that Elena's and Ortiz's identification was accurate and
the Marshes had been lying – the driver of the car had
been Locke.

Unless and until he could identify Locke's motive and be
certain it was strong enough to provoke a fatal assault on

Muir, he had to consider other possible suspects. Jemima's and Grant's motive was money. But believe the evidence he had gained from the bar, Ques, and Ques's woman, and they had an alibi from about 5 in the evening (remembering the time it would take to drive from Port Llueso to Club Gusto) until 4 or 5 in the morning. The medical evidence suggested stabbing had probably occurred 1 to 2 hours before death and death had occurred between 6 at night and 5 in the morning.

Tabitha. She had no known motive unless the row she had had with Muir before she was driven to the port by Ortiz pointed to one.

Vives. He knew Muir was wealthy because he was acting as middleman in the bribery, but there was no evidence to suggest he had ever been anywhere near the house; added to which, he would surely be too scared of receiving violence to inflict it.

The minister. He had everything to gain by receiving the second tranche of the bribe money, everything to lose by hiring a hit man. And why would he do that? Because something had happened to make him fear exposure of his having been bribed? A hit man would have made certain a stabbing was immediately fatal.

Elena or Ortiz. What possible motive could either have had for Muir's death when their continued employment depended on his staying alive? In any case, when they had left Sa Rotaga, Muir had been alive and unharmed and Elena's husband and Ortiz's wife swore both had remained at home from the time of their arrival until the next morning.

What weapon had the attacker used? Forensic had been unable to suggest what it might have been. Could this have been an accident after all? But if so, on what had Muir fallen? Once again, what could have inflicted those wounds and where was it?

Twenty

'I've cooked a Coca d'albercocs,' Dolores said.

Alvarez, seated at the kitchen table, looked up. 'Is it somebody's saint's day?'

'If it were, you obviously would have forgotten whose.' She placed on the table a large plate on which was an open tart; halved and stoned apricots, sprinkled with cinnamon, were set in a sugared pastry base. 'My cousin in Formentera gave me the recipe.'

'I didn't know you had a cousin there.'

'A distant one.'

'Two islands distant.'

She ignored his puerile humour. 'She's not a bad cook, but rates her skills too highly.'

'A common—' He stopped, realizing she might take offence at what he had been going to say.

'What?'

'Someone with your skills wouldn't know that that's quite common.' He cut a large slice of coca, lifted it on to his plate and ate. 'Rename it Coca de ángels,' he said.

She had mixed a mug of hot chocolate and put this down on the table at his side. 'My cousin is inclined to be pig-headed.'

'People from Formentera have always had that reputation.'

'She once insisted one could use chorizo instead of

191

sobrasada in Lomo con col . . . Perhaps the people there do not appreciate the finer points of good cooking.'

'It's not everyone has the privilege that we do in this house.'

'That you enjoy what I cook is obvious; that you begin to appreciate the hours of work it takes is another matter.'

'I couldn't be more appreciative.'

'As my mother used to say, "Words are easily spoken." She was a very wise woman.'

'But a little anti-male . . .'

'You wish to criticize her?'

'I admire her wisdom too much to do that.'

'She also said, "Men are sincere when they praise themselves; when praising others, they have a purpose."'

Her mother had died before he had come to live with her and Jaime – on reflection, he was thankful this was so. 'When I said this coca was good enough for an angel, I meant every word . . .'

'Because you hoped to be offered a second piece?'

'That's not fair.'

'For a man, nothing is fair which is not to his advantage.'

'Another of your mother's sayings?'

'Something I have gleaned from years of living with a husband . . . If you have another slice of coca, make certain it is smaller than the first one. Isabel and Juan will want some when they return.' She swept out of the kitchen.

Why did he so often say the wrong thing or fail to say the right thing? he wondered as he cut himself a second slice, not noticeably smaller than the first. Remember what had happened when he had spoken to Tabitha? He was sure she had hinted she would welcome an invitation, yet he had failed to issue one. Why hadn't he suggested dinner at one of the better restaurants . . . ?

He silently swore. A pair of deep blue eyes had hijacked his wits. Tabitha could steal the heart of any man, yet here he was, imagining she would welcome the attentions of one who was not even the pale shadow of an Adonis, far from clever, and slightly older – an unwelcome honesty compelled him to amend that to considerably older – than she . . .

Dolores's mother would undoubtedly have had a saying to criticize such stupidity, but thankfully he did not know what that was.

Thirty-three minutes later, he made his way up to his office where, short of breath and sweating, he switched on the fan before he slumped down on the chair behind his desk. He tried to find a reason for not phoning Palma and failed.

'Yes?' said Salas.

'It's Inspector Alvarez from Llueso . . .'

'It is not necessary to waste time telling me where you work; nothing could be more evident. What do you want?'

'You told me to report to you after I had questioned the Marshes.'

'Then do so.'

'Señor and Señora Marsh are certain Señor and Señora Locke were at their house throughout the relevant time. If that is true, obviously Señor Locke could not have been driving the car Elena and Ortiz saw and there will on present evidence be no cause to suspect him of any involvement in the death of Señor Muir.'

'Do you doubt the truth of their statements?'

'I believe they were lying.'

'Do you have any proof that they were?'

'No, Señor.'

'Then little weight can be given to your belief.'

193

'It could point the way.'

'In your case, in the opposite direction to that in which one should be proceeding.'

'Yet if it becomes apparent he has a motive for Señor Muir's death—'

'Have you established one?'

'Not yet. But because of information I was possibly given—'

'What the devil do you mean, "possibly given". Either you were or you weren't.'

'It's not quite that straightforward. A rumour was mentioned to me. If that is fact, then there is a very strong motive. I asked England to make enquiries, but unfortunately they have not yet replied. Perhaps they—'

'It did not occur to you it might be logical to confirm the motive before questioning the validity of the alibi?'

'Yes, it did, but you demanded—'

'Efficiency from you. Which speaks of an unbridled optimism . . . I do not remember my giving you permission to request information from England.'

'Well . . . I thought . . .'

'Unlikely. I suppose I shouldn't be surprised by the contemptuous way in which you repeatedly disobey my orders.'

'I decided it would speed things up . . .'

'It is not difficult to suggest what would ensure they were very much more quickly and efficiently carried out . . . When you hear from England, you will get in touch with me immediately. One final thing. Do you remember my warning about pursuing any further enquiries regarding the absurd allegation you had the temerity to make?'

'Yes, Señor.'

'One single word more to anyone and your remaining

time in the Cuerpo will be both brief and inglorious. I trust that is absolutely clear?'

The line went dead.

Alvarez looked at his watch, settled back in the chair and let his thoughts wander. The superior chief's threat loomed large. Any further attempt to prove Muir had been bribing the minister in order to gain planning permission and he would be thrown out of the Cuerpo. Dismissed officers lost their pension rights. With some years to go before he could claim the state pension for those of the third age, he would be penniless unless he found work. Lacking any specialized skills, he would have little chance of gaining employment in the winter; in the summer, it would be easier, but inevitably would mean working in the tourist trade – stacking dirty plates in the sink in a tourist restaurant, serving drinks to drunken tourists . . .

No sooner had he accepted he had no option but to obey Salas's orders than his imagination pictured the Wilderness turned into one more concrete jungle. How could his own future be more important than that of an ancient, almost unspoilt part of the island? To possess the possibility of preventing its desecration and not pursue this, would be an abominable act of cowardice . . . He had to do something because although Muir was dead and the planned development might well not be carried out, the genie had been let out of the bottle and unless it could be crammed back in, development would sooner or later go ahead. Yet wasn't it the law of genies that they only returned to the bottle when willing or tricked into doing so? And as he had asked himself before, what could one insignificant inspector do when ranged against a member of the ruling establishment? . . .

The spirit of defeat passed. There had to be things he could do. For a start, prove the minister a liar, which would damage his reputation (though perhaps not by much since politicians were assumed to be liars). But how to prove he was? . . . The minister had told Salas the money he had spent had come from his unmarried cousin who had lived near Perpignan and died recently. Could this story be shown to be completely false? How near Perpignan had the cousin lived? What did 'died recently' mean in terms of days, weeks, or months? . . . Try asking another police force to identify a person on such ambiguous evidence and the request would be in the waste-paper basket as quickly as it could be thrown. And no Frenchman was ever willing to co-operate with anyone . . .

He was forgetting something more Salas had mentioned. The minister – perhaps nervously trying to appear truthful by offering colourful details – had added that when alive, his cousin had been so poor a cook it was amusing to know his name was the same as a very famous chef. What famous chef? What nationality? Assume the cousin had been French, the chef had also to be French because no other nationality would be considered. Had there been one French chef so famous he became an icon? A name flitted around the edges of his memory and then, as he was about to give up trying to identify it, gained body. Escoffier. Supposedly the inventor of several dishes of great renown. Wasn't one of them Tournedos Rossini? . . .

He spoke on the phone to Directory Enquiries and used his authority – calling himself Comisario – to ask for the telephone number of the Police Judiciaire of the Sûreté Nationale in Perpignan. He dialled the number, spoke to a woman who, having been a Parisian before her marriage, tried not to understand his French, then to a man who was far more helpful and did not even claim the requested enquiries were impossible, but said they would be carried out as soon as possible.

He replaced the receiver. Incredibly, it was only then that he faced the consequences of what he had done. If Salas should ever learn his orders had been ignored within minutes of repeating them . . . How, Alvarez asked himself, could he have allowed sentiment to put him on the road to disaster? Was there any way of undoing what he had done? . . . In a growing panic, desperate to find a measure of reassurance, he opened the bottom right-hand drawer of the desk, found only the empty bottle which he had intended to take home in a plastic bag, not wanting the members of the Guardia to think he drank during working hours, and replace it with a full one . . .

Life could become a bottomless pit of blackness.

Twenty-One

On Friday morning, Alvarez arrived in his office, sat, and stared at the telephone on his desk. Would it ring, would the plum-voiced secretary tell him Salas wanted to speak to him? . . .

How could he have been so pleased with himself for working out the possible surname of the minister's cousin that he had acted with uncharacteristic impulsiveness? Why had he got in touch with the Police Judiciare directly so that it would be his name which was marked down as the originator of the requested enquiries?

The phone did ring, causing him to start and his heart to beat more quickly. It occurred to him that if he suffered a sudden heart attack, he would not be called to account – but that did seem rather a drastic solution to the problem. He finally reached out for the receiver.

'Inspector Alvarez,' he said in a croaky voice.

'Barry here. How's yourself, what's the weather like and if it's hot and sunny, don't tell me.'

Initially, the release from tension on finding the speaker was not Salas was so great he understood no more than that the other was speaking English. Then he calmed and identified Barry Denton, whom he'd asked to make enquiries regarding Zara Locke. 'It's raining heavily and almost as cold as mid-winter.'

'I wish I could believe that because it would make our

appalling summer more bearable . . . First off, apologies for being so long getting back to you, but the enquiries turned out to be more difficult than expected.'

'I'm sorry if I've given you a great deal of work.'

'Think nothing of it until I do the same to you . . . The upshot of things is that I've some information which I'll send on by fax.'

'Do you think it will help?'

'I'd say it might very well do so if it can be proved Locke knew Muir's nickname was Dinty.'

'A woman told me Señor Locke learned that at Muir's party and he and his wife were so upset, they left very soon afterwards . . . Can you very briefly tell me what the evidence is?'

'Zara Locke worked for a firm of solicitors. She kept a diary and in this recorded meeting an older, wealthy man called Dinty – she never mentions another name – with whom she first became emotionally involved, then physically. Having bedded her, he dumped her and moved on – obviously, a man who enjoys the chase is bored by the capture. She became so depressed – a depression probably fuelled by the drug habit to which he had introduced her – that she committed suicide. Enquiries were made to try to identify Dinty, but these never met any success.'

Alvarez said slowly: 'So at the party, Señor Locke learned who was responsible for his daughter's death.'

'Just a warning. According to the books, Dinty is a common nickname for someone called Muir. I suppose there might be a coincidence here?'

'Señor Muir was notorious for pursuing women and then quickly discarding them so I don't suppose there was a moment's doubt in Señor Locke's mind. And what father would not want to gain his revenge on such a man even though he realizes that if he succeeds, he may be accused of murder?'

'You don't think he should be?'

'Do you not meet cases where your sympathies are with the guilty persons?'

'Emotional sympathy, maybe, professional sympathy, no. An eye for an eye can only lead to anarchy.'

Alvarez did not argue. Perhaps Barry Denton always worked within the rules and never acknowledged the possibility that justice could occasionally breed injustice. He apologized again for the trouble he had caused, thanked the other for all the work he'd done, prophesied the case was as good as solved.

He replaced the receiver. What was his next move? Did he face Locke with the new evidence or first question the Marshes to try to destroy the alibi they were providing? He decided to speak to the Marshes first. And on the way to their home, he could stop off at Club Llueso and have his merienda which, due to the stress of work, had been delayed.

'You again!' Raquel said as, having opened the front door of Ca'n Bastoyne, she faced Alvarez.

'I need to have another word with Señor and Señora Marsh.'

'You can't talk to her, she's shopping.'

Life wasn't all about disappointment, he thought, as he stepped into the hall. Marsh was the weaker of the two and perhaps might suffer from the strange English custom of telling the truth to authority.

Alvarez entered the sitting room. 'Good morning, Señor.'

Marsh's consternation was obvious. After looking at the door to the patio, as if contemplating running to it, he said nervously: 'My wife isn't here so—'

'It is you I wish to speak to.'

'Why?'

'There are one or two questions I have to ask you.'

'I can't tell you anything more than I already have.'

'I am hoping you will find you can.'

'Look, I'm sorry, but I'm meant to be going out to have coffee with friends . . .'

'Then I will be as brief as possible.'

'Couldn't you come back some other time?'

'I am afraid not.'

Marsh said weakly: 'In that case . . . would you like a drink?'

'Thank you.'

He hurried out of the room. A moment later, Alvarez heard the front door being opened, then shut as Marsh looked to see if his wife was in sight. He reappeared. 'I didn't ask what you wanted?'

'A coñac with just ice, please.'

Marsh left, carefully closed the door. The minutes passed. Alvarez was not surprised. Despite his previous claim to be in a hurry, Marsh was delaying the questioning as long as he dare in the hope his wife would return in time to support him. With luck, she would have a long shopping list.

He finally returned, carrying two glasses, handed one to Alvarez, sat, immediately drank. 'There really is nothing more I know.'

'Señor, it will be best if I explain first why it must be in your interests to correct anything you have previously told me which was wrong. You must understand that the demands of friendship can sometimes carry too heavy a price.'

'I . . . I don't know what that means.'

'If a friend asks for help, naturally one gives it; if the

friendship is strong, one sometimes does so even when knowing one shouldn't. Wouldn't you agree?'

'I . . . Maybe, but . . .'

'Of course, it can happen that it's obvious one shouldn't have done as asked only after doing it. That is the point at which one must realize friendship can demand too great a price.'

There was a silence, which Alvarez did not break for a while – guilt blossomed in silence. Finally, he said: 'Naturally, Spanish jails are run humanely, but I understand it might be considered conditions are less rigorous in Britain. And for a foreigner there is, of course, the additional penalty of becoming the butt of those stupid enough to find differences in speech, customs, and manners, to be cause for persecution; to the extent that sometimes he has to be kept in solitary confinement for his own safety and that can have peculiar effects.'

'Why are you saying all this?' Marsh demanded hoarsely.

'Because you have to understand the consequences of lying to the police . . . Señor, I have lived through difficult times and these teach one more about life and people than do good times. I have learned that a man may break the law for a reason most would consider admirable, but because the law has to set up boundaries, it will condemn him. This is why I believe there is often reason to allow someone to have second thoughts before arresting him. I was here yesterday morning and I asked your wife and you . . . Perhaps it will be fairer if I first tell you I have come into possession of further evidence.'

Marsh drained his glass. He was sweating even though the room was cooled by an air-conditioning unit set high up on a wall.

'Evidence which makes it quite clear Señor and Señora

Locke could not have had tea and spent part of the evening with you that Saturday.' Would his bluff work? Had his earlier words and implied threats sufficiently weakened any resolve Marsh might have had? 'Señor, if I hear the truth now, I shall forget the lies I have previously been told because they were spoken in the name of friendship.'

There was a long pause before Marsh said weakly: 'What do you want to know?'

'On Saturday, the thirteenth, did Señor and Señora Locke unexpectedly arrive here whilst you were still enjoying a siesta?'

Marsh swallowed heavily. 'Scott couldn't . . . couldn't kill anyone.'

'Circumstances more often promote murder than character.'

'Laura said—' He stopped.

'What did Señora Locke say?'

'I need another drink.' Marsh stood, picked up his glass, hurried out of the room. When he returned, he sat and stared at the carpet.

'Neither Señor Locke nor Señora Locke came here that Saturday afternoon, did they?' Alvarez spoke with quiet certainty.

Marsh drank. He began to speak, became silent, drank again. Finally, nervously and disjointedly, he said that no, no one had visited them that afternoon whilst they had been enjoying their siesta. Some days later, Keir had arrived, obviously in a state of uneasy excitement, and told them it seemed Scott's death had not been a straightforward accident. Which put him, Keir, in a very embarrassing position because if Scott had been murdered, obviously one of the police's first moves would be to identify anyone who had visited Sa Rotaga in the hours before his death. The fact was, he had driven up there in the

late afternoon and had passed a car in which he thought
had been the two staff. Since identification made from one
car passing another was seldom reliable, as evidenced by
his uncertainty that they really had been the staff, it was
very possible that neither of them had been able to identify
him; however, if they believed they had, they would tell the
police who would be almost bound to come to the wrong
conclusion . . . He had not seen or spoken to Scott. He'd
knocked on the front door, rung the bell, to no avail, had
left and returned home . . . So to avoid any unpleasantness,
he'd asked them, in the name of friendship and trust, to give
him an alibi if ever called upon to do so; had even detailed
what that alibi should be . . .

'You immediately agreed?'

'Not immediately, no. In fact . . . Well, I didn't want to
because . . .'

Because he could foresee the consequences if the lie was
ever exposed?

'But in the end, Evelyn . . . We agreed to do it.'

'You never doubted Señor Locke had nothing to do with
Señor Muir's death?'

'Of course we didn't.'

'Why not?'

'You've only got to know him to be certain he would
never deliberately hurt anyone.'

'Even when he had the strongest reason to hate?'

'You . . . you know about their daughter?'

'Yes.'

'He still wouldn't.'

'Has he ever made any comment to you about Señor
Muir's death?'

'Only . . .'

'Yes?'

'It's nothing.'

'I still need to know what he said.'

'Only . . . Anyone would say the same thing, wouldn't he?'

'Until I know what was said, I cannot answer.'

'Whoever did kill Scott deserved a medal . . . But that doesn't mean that he . . . You must understand.'

'Señor, I understand that you are a good friend and therefore find it impossible to believe he might seek revenge for his daughter's death.'

'But you can?'

'It is my job to consider any and all possibilities.'

'There isn't a nicer person on the island.'

'I will not forget that you have said that.' Alvarez stood. 'Thank you for helping me, Señor.'

'I wish . . .'

'I know what you wish. But the truth had to be told eventually.'

'It's made me feel like a damned informer.'

Alvarez said goodbye and left; Marsh made no attempt to follow him. As he stepped out of the house, a red Peugeot drove in and came to a stop, so abruptly that the tyres briefly slid on the loose gravel. Evelyn opened the door and climbed out. 'Why are you here again?' she demanded angrily.

'I needed to ask your husband some more questions, which he has kindly answered.'

She muttered something he judged to be unladylike, hurried past him and into the house. Her husband, he thought, as he climbed into the Ibiza, was about to regret his honesty.

Twenty-Two

Alvarez drove slowly, ignoring the driver of the car behind who was flashing the headlights to try to make him speed up. It was a quarter to one. Three-quarters of an hour before he needed to be back home if he were to enjoy a brandy before lunch. So did he wait to question the Lockes until the afternoon? The more time that passed, the more likely the Marshes would decide to tell them what had happened and that their alibi had been destroyed. So did he heed duty or pleasure? Slightly surprised by his decision, he continued to the crossroads and then turned right to drive along the lane and the dirt track to Ca Na Aila.

Beatriz said the señor and señora were out by the pool and led him through the cool sitting room to the covered patio. Locke stood, shook hands, and asked what he'd like to drink, Laura greeted him with a smile and the hope he was well.

As Beatriz returned indoors, they sat. Locke said: 'So what brings you here, Inspector?'

'As always, Señor, more questions.'

'That suggests you've still no idea who stabbed Scott?'

'I have an idea. My present task is to decide if it is correct.'

'You think we can help you do that?' Laura asked.

'I am not certain.'

'You seem uncertain about many things.'

206

'Steady on, Laura,' Locke said lightly. 'After all, it's odds on that in the inspector's work there are always very many more possibilities than probabilities . . . Isn't that right?'

'It is very true,' Alvarez agreed.

'But we've told you before, we can't help you,' she snapped.

Locke looked quickly at her, worried by her obvious uneasiness.

'Señora, it quite often happens that a person believes he cannot help an investigation and therefore naturally resents being questioned time after time, but suddenly, and to his own surprise, a forgotten memory is recovered and he learns he can after all assist.'

'There aren't any memories we could have forgotten.'

'Then I shall not have to trouble you for very long.'

Beatriz came out on to the patio and put a glass on the table in front of Alvarez, returned inside.

'Your good health,' Locke said, as he raised his half-empty glass. Laura did and said nothing, her expression hard and unfriendly.

Once again, a very good brandy, Alvarez noted approvingly.

'Well?' Laura demanded. 'What do you want us to try to remember?'

He turned to Locke. 'Señor, when I was here before, you told me that on the Saturday you and the señora visited your friends, the Marshes, and had tea there.'

'It was I who told you that, not Keir,' Laura said sharply.

'Of course. Forgive me . . . Señora, would you like to alter your evidence?'

'Why the hell should I want to?'

'Perhaps if it was not the truth.'

207

'Are you trying to call me a liar?'

'Laura—' Locke began.

'Don't tell me I musn't say that. If he's calling me a liar, I'm bloody well going to object. I told him what happened and that was the truth.'

'I'm afraid not, Señora.'

'If you're going to go on insulting me, you'd better leave.'

'Before coming here, I spoke to Señor Marsh again.'

She picked up her glass and drained it. She stared out at the pool, her features drawn tight by fear.

'I asked him to confirm what he had previously told me. He then admitted both he and his wife had been lying because they had been asked to do so. They were not visited by anyone that afternoon or evening.'

Laura reached out and put her hand on her husband's arm, suddenly realized that a significance might be drawn from her action, snatched her hand away.

'Señor,' Alvarez said, 'did you drive to Sa Rotaga that Saturday afternoon?'

'He was with me, here,' she said wildly.

'Laura—'

'You were here, with me. We never moved from here, either of us.' She faced Alvarez. 'All right, I made up the story about arriving at Evelyn's with a cake.'

'Why did you do that?'

'Isn't it obvious? You came here with the crazy story Keir had driven up to Scott's place; I had to do something.'

'I think, Señora, you had to do something because you were scared it really was your husband who had killed Señor Muir.'

'I know he couldn't have done because he was here all the time. Why won't you understand? He couldn't have been there because he was here.' Her voice rose until she was almost shouting. 'In God's name, why would he want to kill Scott?'

'I know about the tragedy of your daughter.'

'Oh, Christ!' Tears welled out of her eyes and ran down her cheeks.

'I did not kill Scott,' Locke said harshly.

'You had the strongest of motives since, at the party, you finally learned the probable identity of the man who had ruined your daughter's life and driven her tragically to commit suicide.'

'All right, I hated his guts. And maybe I had fantasized about gaining revenge, but that's all it amounted to, fantasy. If you want the truth, I hadn't the guts to kill him.'

'You drove to his house that afternoon.'

'Why can't you understand what I keep telling you?' she demanded violently. 'He was here, here.'

'Señorita, he was recognized by the staff, driving up to Sa Rotaga.'

'They're lying.'

'Why should they lie?'

'How could I know why?'

Alvarez spoke to Locke. 'Did you drive to Sa Rotaga that afternoon?'

'He didn't, he didn't.' She again reached out to her husband, to seek and to give emotional help, and in doing so, began to tip the chair. Locke quickly supported this and then pushed it back to an upright position. She began to make a sound at the back of her throat which was a cry of overwhelming fear.

Alvarez hesitated, then stood. 'I must not bring you even more distress, so I will leave.'

He looked at the phone. He lit a cigarette. He wished

time would race and release him but, as always, it did the opposite to what was wanted and the seconds dragged. A man could curse his fate, but never avoid it. He finally rang Palma and was told to wait. Receiver to ear, he watched a gecko near the window. If he were a gecko, would his life be made miserable by a superior gecko?

'Yes?' Salas snapped.

'Señor, I have—'

'Who are you?'

'Inspector Alvarez.'

'Then why the devil don't you say so? Do you expect me to know by instinct who's calling?'

'But the last time I phoned you, you strongly objected when I named myself—'

'Nonsense! What do you want?'

'I have spoken to Señor and Señora Marsh and they have admitted their previous evidence was false. The Lockes did not arrive at their house that Saturday afternoon and stay until after supper. In view of this, I questioned Señor Locke again and put it to him that he had been lying. Actually, it was his wife who originally claimed they had visited the Marshes . . .'

'What did he say?'

'Very little because his wife repeatedly said that yes, she had lied, they had not gone to the Marshes, but her husband had been at home all the time. Her behaviour revealed just how scared she was on his behalf because she knew he had driven to Sa Rotaga. She believed it must have been he who had attacked Muir . . . But even if he had the most powerful of motives, even if she fears he was the attacker, I find it difficult to believe he was.'

'Why?'

'His character. He's too open and straightforward a person. He'd have used his fists, not some kind of weapon.

And he was described to me as one of the most decent and honourable persons on the island.'

'Hardly a commendation of consequence if the comparison is with other foreigners. I find it astonishing that an officer in my command should present evidence which seemingly inescapably points to a person's guilt, then assures me that person is not guilty solely on the grounds of character.'

'It's difficult to explain . . .'

'You have not arrested him?'

'No.'

'Because you prefer an emotional judgement to hard evidence? Let there be the strongest of motives, proof the suspect was in the vicinity of the victim in the envelope of relevant time, an attempt to concoct a false alibi, and all that becomes irrelevant when set against your judgement of his character?'

'Sometimes one gets the feeling—'

'Indeed. And your conduct in this case has given me the feeling that you have become virtually incapable of carrying out your job, even in your usual incompetent manner . . . Had you but a modicum of professional ability, by now Locke would be under arrest.'

'The evidence certainly points to him, but there just isn't enough evidence as yet to warrant his arrest. And then—'

'I will hear nothing more about character. The lack of sufficient evidence is easily explained. You have spent most of your time and effort pursuing slanderous fantasies instead of the case in hand.'

'The money in the safe had to be explained.'

'Not in a manner that resulted in an honourable man being insulted.'

'I am still convinced he was bribed.'

'Your conviction is almost certainly proof of his complete innocence.'

'Why were the initials—'

'You will not repeat nonsense.'

There was a silence.

'Have you nothing more to say?' Salas finally asked.

'I don't think so, Señor.'

'You cannot suggest how you intend uncovering the further evidence you deem necessary to arrest Locke?'

'If it could be shown beyond question that no one else connected with the case had the slightest motive for assaulting him . . . But it is always very difficult to prove a negative.'

'So naturally you have not attempted to do so.'

'Señor, I have already questioned all those with any conceivable motive of which I am aware and I am satisfied they are in the clear; but, of course, that is not to say it is impossible for them—'

'Who have you questioned?'

'Señora Muir and her toy boy—'

'Her what?'

'The man she is with is considerably younger than she. Obviously she came to the island expecting to be able to blackmail Señor Muir, but she discovered once again that he'd been too smart for her. That left her in financial trouble which made it likely her bed would go cold—'

'What has her bed to do with anything?'

'If she'd no money, Grant would stop servicing her and move on to more profitable beds.'

'Your ability to invest any and every relationship with a demeaning sexual content is quite extraordinary.'

There was no point in trying to explain. Was Salas's absurd prudery due to repressed desires? . . . Not a thought to pursue. 'So on the face of things, she had a strong motive.

But I've checked their alibi and they did spend the late afternoon and evening at a bar and the club and—'

'Where?'

'Club Gusto.'

'I have never heard of it.'

'I should say that that is hardly surprising.'

'You are trying to be insulting?'

'Far from it, Señor. The club is notorious for the type of entertainment it provides.'

'Which is what?'

'I don't think you'd wish to know . . .'

'Would I ask if I didn't?'

'The live show involves couples, or perhaps more people, naked and—'

'I will not have you encouraging your delight in the sordid.'

'But you said—'

'Enough!'

'I questioned staff at the bar to which they went beforehand and at the club and there's no doubt the two of them were at one or other place from late afternoon until well after midnight and he certainly became too drunk to attack anyone. Since a person can't be in two places at the same time—'

'Remarkable that you should reach a logical conclusion. Has it occurred to you the staff might have been bribed to provide a false alibi?'

'I strongly doubt that possibility.'

'You do not consider it worthwhile checking out your doubts?'

'It would take a long time—'

'When you have better things to do, such as unwarranted enquiries into the affairs of a person I am not going to name? Let you attempt to pursue those one iota further,

Alvarez, and you will no longer be a member of the
Cuerpo.' He cut the connexion.

Alvarez thought about enquiries now going on near
Perpignan. He brought out the unopened bottle of Soberano
and a glass, unscrewed the cap and poured himself a very
large brandy . . .

Twenty-Three

Dolores said, as she stood by the dining-room table and studied Alvarez: 'You look very tired and worried. Are you not feeling well?' Her concern was sharp. She watched over her family's well-being with an even sharper eye than she observed their faults.

'I'm fine,' he replied.

'You've hardly said a word since you got back.'

'Wouldn't you say that's an advantage?' asked Jaime, with a smirk.

'An advantage you forever deny us,' she snapped.

'I've had a very heavy day,' Alvarez said.

'You must tell your superior chief he is overworking you.'

'He wouldn't listen.'

'Make him. Even if he is a Madridleño, he should be capable of understanding you must have time to relax.' She crossed to the bead curtain and went through to the kitchen.

'You overworking?' Jaime sniggered. 'That's good for a laugh.'

There was a call from the kitchen. 'A fool laughs at his own faults.'

Jaime spoke in a low voice. 'She's got ears a metre long.' He emptied his glass and was about to pick up the bottle of wine when he checked his hand. 'Here,

are you sure you don't feel ill? You've hardly drunk
anything.'

'I've been thinking.'

'About running your hands under the skirt of the woman
you've been seeing?'

'Tell me something. If you had a daughter—'

'What are you on about? I have a daughter.'

'If you had a daughter in her early twenties, an only
child, and she meets a man who uses his charm, money, and
drugs, to bed her and having succeeded, chucks her aside
because it's the chase which really interests him, and she's
become so emotionally involved, she commits suicide,
what would you do to that man when you had the chance?'

'Slit his throat, cut off his cojones and feed 'em to the
pigs . . . No, that's wrong. I'd cut 'em off before I slit his
throat so as he knew what was happening.'

'In the old days, maybe, but not now because—'

His words were cut short by Dolores as she pushed her
way through the bead curtain. 'Why should a father not
now behave honourably?'

'He'd be called a murderer.'

'By whom?'

'The law.'

'Does the law not understand how a father feels who
loses a daughter to such a man?'

'It's concerned with people's actions, not their emotions.'

'Then it is small wonder to find what kind of person
becomes a lawyer . . . Is this the problem which is making
you look so tired?'

'Yes.'

'There is such a father?'

'There is.'

'And did he cut off the seducer's cojones and slit his
throat?'

'He just stabbed him.'

'Men have become so weak.'

'When I uncover the final proof, I must charge him with killing the seducer.'

'He will be imprisoned?'

'Of course.'

'Stupidity haunts the world since it is men who make the laws! What are you going to do?'

'What can I do but my job? But never have I wished to do anything less.'

'No wonder you are so worried. Empty your glass and refill it.'

'I don't think a couple of bottles would really help.'

'Perhaps not, but they would lessen your misery. So drink up . . . I must continue cooking or we will have nothing to eat.' She hurried back into the kitchen.

Jaime stared at the bead curtain, the strands of which slowly came to rest. 'You look tired and complain about the job and she says, drink, drink. If I looked tired and complained about my job, she'd tell me my trouble was, I drink too much.' He once more reached across to the bottle of wine.

'Jaime,' she called out.

He snatched his hand away.

'Come here.'

'Why?'

'To collect some things to put on the table.'

'The kids can do that.'

'It has escaped your notice they are not here because they are having supper with Susana?'

'Can't you bring them in, then?'

She pushed her way through the bead curtain for the second time to stand with her arms across her bosom. 'You have more important things to do than to help me?'

217

'That's not—'

'Drinking being one of them?'

'That's not—'

'Kindly come and get the things.' She unfolded her arms and swept back into the kitchen.

Muttering angrily – while making certain his words could not be heard – he stood, pushed back his chair, and crossed to the kitchen.

Alvarez took hold of his glass, but instead of raising it and drinking, began slowly to turn it around. What right had he to set himself up as a judge? Locke had stabbed Muir because Muir was guilty of an abominable crime; apparently, justice had been done . . . But did he know all the facts? Could there be motives and therefore possible suspects still hidden from him? Surely not . . .

There was a shout of pain from the kitchen. He came to his feet and hurried through, to find Jaime swearing as he held out his left hand for Dolores to examine. 'What's happened?'

'He's cut himself,' she said. She released his hand.

'I'm bleeding most terribly,' Jaime cried.

'Put your hand under the cold tap – that'll slow the bleeding . . . Enrique, get a plaster and the Cinfacromin.'

As she propelled Jaime across to the sink, Alvarez picked up the lid of the plastic box marked with a red cross and brought out a small bottle of antiseptic and a roll of sticking plaster.

She turned on the cold tap, told Jaime to put his middle finger under the water.

'It's a bloody deep cut,' Jaime cried.

'I don't think so, cariño.'

'If the knife was dirty, I'll be infected.'

'The knife was clean.'

'I'll need a blood transfusion.'

'The bleeding is already diminishing.'

'They'll have to stitch the wound. I couldn't stand them pushing a needle through my skin; it makes me feel faint just to think about it.'

She straightened up. 'Then stop thinking about it.' Her tone was no longer concerned. 'There'll be no need to stitch anything since it's only a shallow cut.'

'Shallow? I felt the knife dig into my bone . . .'

'Only in your imagination. Keep your finger under the tap for a little longer, then dry it and put on some Cinfacromin and a plaster. Or get Enrique to do it for you if that would make you feel faint,' she added sarcastically.

'There's real sympathy for you!'

'In what words should one sympathize with a man who nicks a finger to draw a little blood, then shouts he is dying? Sweet Mary, but what my mother said is so true. "A woman is born to endure pain and suffering in silence, a man to shout if he so much as pricks himself . . ." The moment the plaster's on, you can both clear out of here so I can finish cooking the meal.' She faced Jaime. 'I presume you'll be feeling too shocked to eat anything?'

Minutes later, he and Alvarez sat once more at the dining-room table.

'How was I to know I hadn't cut my artery and was bleeding to death?' Jaime asked resentfully, as he refilled his glass.

Alvarez told himself there was no reason to choose to question Tabitha before others, but knew he was lying. He could not forget how she had asked him if his words were an invitation and he had failed to pursue the possibility there had been an invitation in her words.

The clerk on duty at the reception desk at Hotel Terramar

told him Tabitha had returned to the hotel very recently with her friend and they had gone up to their room.

'See if they're still there, will you?'

After speaking over the phone, the clerk passed across the receiver.

'Miss Telfer, it's Inspector Alvarez. May I have a word with you?'

'More than one, I hope.'

'Then would you like to come down . . .'

'It will be much quieter up here in our room.'

It would be far more sensible to speak to her in a public area. 'All right,' he heard himself say.

He handed back the receiver. 'Which room is she in?'

'Twenty-nine,' the clerk answered immediately.

Alvarez ironically wondered if any other room number was fixed in the clerk's memory? 'That's on the second floor?'

'Right . . . Going up, are you?'

'And if I am?'

There was no answer.

Alvarez crossed to the lift. On the second floor, he walked to the end of the right-hand corridor, knocked on the door of No. 29. There was a call to enter.

Tabitha, wearing a brightly coloured cotton frock, was sitting on the left-hand bed, her back resting against the wall; Mary sat at a small table by the single window. He said good morning, careful to make it clear he was greeting both of them.

'Hullo, again, Inspector. Or am I allowed to call you Enrique?' Tabitha asked.

No woman, he thought, should be so immediately attractive that a man's mind spun; no woman should appear to be both innocent and sexually intriguing. 'Call me what you like.'

220

'You don't think that's a dangerous permission to give?'

'I hope not, Miss Telfer . . .'

'Is your memory so very short? I'm Tabitha.'

'I should like to ask you a few more questions.'

'Then you're here on duty, not for pleasure?'

He decided it was a moment for heavy gallantry. 'A little duty and, hopefully, a lot of pleasure.'

'Then perhaps I will answer at least some of your questions.'

Mary stood. 'I'm going to post my cards.'

Alvarez said: 'Perhaps you should stay here, Señorita.'

'Why? I told you last time I couldn't help you and nothing's changed, so where's the point?'

'Perhaps,' Tabitha said, 'Enrique thinks I need chaperoning.'

'Then he'll be the first man to make that mistake.' Mary faced Alvarez. 'Are you saying I can't leave?'

'No, only that if you stay, you might remember something that will help me.'

'I won't.' She picked up a small handbag, walked out of the room and slammed the door behind herself.

'Sometimes she can be very difficult,' Tabitha said.

'Is it because I am here?'

'Why should that disturb her?'

'I've no idea.'

'Then it can't be anything to do with you, can it? She's just in one of her moods . . . Are you going to go on standing?'

She had moved her hand as she spoke and for one wild moment, he imagined she had touched the bed to suggest he sat by her side. Sanity returned. He crossed to the single chair. 'During the time you were with Señor Muir—'

'Do we have to talk about him?'

221

'I'm afraid so.'

'Why?'

'Because I am investigating his death . . .'

'But you said you were here for pleasure. Remembering him is the opposite to pleasure.'

'I think I suggested I had to mix pleasure with duty.'

'It would sound nicer if you said, mix duty with pleasure.'

'Did he ever talk to you about any of the other British who live here?'

'I'd say, he normally had only one topic of conversation. But I don't think I'll tell you what that was because it might embarrass me.'

'Did he ever mention the name of Keir Locke?'

'I don't think so.'

'Or Zara Locke?'

'No. Who's she?'

'A young woman who fell in love with him and then committed suicide when he threw her aside.'

'She didn't realize what a bastard he was?'

'Why do you call him that?'

'Tell the truth and shame the devil.'

'Yet you were very friendly with him.'

'You've never learned that a bastard can have quite an attraction for a lady . . . Mary is quite right. She says you're not very worldly . . . Oh! I shouldn't have told you that. Now you'll be annoyed.'

'I've been described in far more unflattering terms. Señora Muir is here with a friend called Lawrence Grant—'

She interrupted him. 'Don't you want to know why she said that?'

'Not really.'

'Then I'll tell you. It's because you didn't take my hint the other day. I said you weren't unworldly, just a wonderfully old-fashioned kind of husband, too loyal to do anything that might upset your wife.'

'I am not married.'

'Then perhaps you just didn't want . . . Let's forget it.'

'I didn't say anything because I found it difficult to believe you would welcome an invitation from me.'

'Why shouldn't I?'

This was not a moment for caution. 'Can I make up for my slowness? Will you have dinner with me tonight?'

'I was beginning to fear you'd never ask.'

Her smile was so warm that it was some time before he resumed questioning her. He learned nothing new. After Ortiz had driven her back to the hotel, she and Mary had spent the remainder of the afternoon and the early evening on the beach, then they had had dinner.

In his office, Alvarez reached across to the telephone, lifted the receiver and dialled.

'Llueso Villas,' a woman said.

'Is Angel there?'

'Who's speaking?'

'Enrique Alvarez.'

After a brief pause, a man said: 'Enrique, you old sod, fancy hearing from you this early in the day!' Vadell was full of bounce and jokes in dubious taste; he was a lecher, wealthy, and a man in whom it was dangerous to place a scintilla of trust.

'I'm ringing to ask a favour.'

'Anything for an old pal.'

'You own and manage a lot of villas. I'd like to borrow one for tonight.'

'Are you serious? It's in the middle of the season and they're all full.'

'Then how about Ca'n Amarillo?'

Some seconds passed before Vadell said: 'There's nowhere with that name on my books.'

'Probably not, but your firm will be paying all the bills, even if it's officially owned by a nephew to keep the tax people quiet.'

'Are you working for those bastards now?'

'No.'

'Then get your nose out of my business.'

'I've heard you keep the place so that you can discreetly entertain friends.'

'Then you've been listening to a load of crap.'

'It's to be hoped the rumours don't reach Carolina's ears or I'm sure she'd be very upset. Especially as there are those who say it's largely her money which supports your business.'

'Are you trying to blackmail me into letting you use my place?' Vadell shouted.

'I'd prefer to use the word, persuade.'

'Of course you would, being a bloody hypocrite.'

There was a silence.

'I'd be very grateful,' Alvarez said finally.

'You can be as grateful as you like, forget it.'

'You'll be entertaining rather a lot in the near future? Then it's to be hoped Carolina remains happily ignorant of the fact.'

'If I ever . . . Just tonight?'

'I'm not so certain. A man can get lucky.'

'Not if he knows you, he bloody can't.'

'I'll call in to pick up the keys. There's one last thing.'

'What?'

'Is the drinks' cupboard well stocked?'

'You want a ten-piece orchestra as well?'

Alvarez said goodbye and replaced the receiver. Life was usually sweeter when one had good friends.

Twenty-Four

Alvarez stepped through the bead curtain into the kitchen. Dolores, sweating, was stirring the contents of a greixonera on the stove. He cleared his throat. 'I won't—'

'Pass me the paprika.'

He looked at the table, on which were several small glass containers of spices, half a cabbage, skinned garlic, a bottle of olive oil, and slices of pan moreno. 'Which is the paprika?'

She put the wooden spoon down, crossed to the table, picked up one of the glass containers. 'Ask a man to help in the kitchen and suddenly he cannot tell a tomato from a carrot.'

'How am I supposed to know which of those contains paprika?'

'You could always try reading the labels.' She unscrewed the cap, sprinkled some of the powder over the contents of the greixonera.

He cleared his throat for a second time.

'Since you are no more use in here than an empty butano canister, you can go out and leave me to work.'

'I wanted to tell you I won't be in to supper.'

She put the paprika container down on the table with far more force than was necessary. 'He will not be eating here, he says! How strange when only a short while ago he asked me to make another sopes because he liked it so much he couldn't eat it too often. And did he not try to ingratiate himself by saying a sopes I made was twice as delicious as any other? So even though this is the heart of the summer and every minute in a kitchen is exhausting, I decided I would suffer in order to grant him his request. Fool that I was! Why did I forget that the tongue which flicks the fastest is the serpent's?'

'I don't remember asking you to make sopes again.'

'Of course you don't. It is so easy to forget when it is someone else who has to do all the work . . . Aiyee! A woman's life is one long, unrewarded sacrifice.'

'If I'd known you thought—'

'How would that have made any difference since you, as any other man, is concerned only with yourself?' She stopped stirring. 'I wonder what it is that creeps into a man's mind and persuades him a woman less than half his age will not notice his hair is receding, his teeth are yellowing—'

'My hair is not receding and my teeth are white.'

'—his skin is blotchy, his breath is tainted, his shoulders are bowed, his belly is sagging—'

'Why don't you shove me in a coffin and have done with it? . . . This morning, I met a man with whom I was at training college and hadn't seen since then. We've a whole lot to talk about and since he's only on the island for a very short time, we decided to meet again this evening. I know I didn't tell you earlier I would not be in for supper, but—'

'When a man takes the trouble to explain in detail, one can be certain he is lying.' She resumed stirring. 'I presume you are meeting that naked woman again?'

'I am not and she was not naked.'

'Were that true, then you would have imagined her naked; since she was naked, you now imagine her clothed.

226

It is not difficult to understand a man's mind if one remembers that rats rarely walk in straight lines.'

He wondered if an abject apology might melt a little of the ice. 'I really am very sorry if there's been a misunderstanding about tonight—'

'For me, there is a complete understanding.'

'But you seem to think—'

'My thoughts concern only myself.'

It was hopeless. 'I'll be off very shortly.'

'Will you return before you start work on Monday?'

'I'll be back tonight.'

'You fear that what you have to say to your friend from the training school may not cement your relationship?'

He left the kitchen.

'That was perfect, Enrique,' Tabitha said as they drove out of the restaurant car park. 'Delicious food, gorgeous wine, and perfect company.' She briefly touched his right arm in a gesture of affection.

The bill had been considerably larger than expected, but he consoled himself with the thought that only a small mind would cavil at the cost.

'Where now?' she asked.

Then she wasn't expecting to be driven straight back to the hotel and he wouldn't be called upon to suggest why she shouldn't. 'I thought it would be fun to go to Parelona. I've a friend with a villa overlooking the bay and when the sky's clear and there's a full moon, I call it a slice of heaven.'

'Won't it be a little late to arrive?'

'He's away on holiday with his family, so the place is empty.'

'Can one swim?'

'It's the best swimming on the island.'

She laughed.

'May I share the joke?'

'For you, everything is the best on the island, which means in the world.' She touched his arm again, a little longer this time. 'I'm not laughing at you, Enrique, but with you. It's so nice to hear someone being fiercely proud of where he lives . . . So I'm going to enjoy the best swim on the island!'

The villa stood ten metres above the level of the sea, almost directly opposite Hotel Parelona on the other side of the bay. Several yachts were anchored and one of them had strung coloured lights from bows to masthead to stern. The sky was cloudless, the moon full; the air was tinged with the scent of wild thyme and rosemary; a nightingale sang a solitary song and then was joined by a companion.

'You were wrong,' she said. 'This isn't a slice of heaven, it is heaven.'

He looked across the patio at the chaise longue on which she lay. In the moonlight, she was more beautiful, more innocent, yet more sensually desirable than ever. He picked up the glass by the side of his chair and drank, too tense to notice the quality of Vadell's brandy.

'If I go swimming in the moonlight, will I turn into a mermaid?'

'I hope not.'

'That's what I was told when I was a small girl. And ever since then, I've wondered. Isn't it crazy how something lasts through one's life even when one knows it's nonsense?' She stood in one easy movement. 'I can't wait to find out if the water's as velvety as it looks . . . Oh, Lord! I've just realized.'

That she had no costume?

'We haven't any towels.'

'There are bound to be some somewhere.'

'Your friend won't mind our using them?'

'I'll take them home to clean and dry, then return them.'

'Shall we start looking?'

In a cupboard in one of the bedrooms were several gaily patterned beach towels. She picked up the top one. 'I'll get out of my clothes in the nearest bathroom.'

He undressed in a second bathroom, wrapped a towel around his waist. He waited in the sitting room for less than a minute before she entered. She had fixed her towel immediately above her breasts and it reached down to just below her buttocks. In a bikini, more of her body had been visible, but to see her now, assuming she was naked underneath the towel, was far more erotic . . .

He led the way out on to the patio and down wooden steps to the small landing stage.

'Do you think the water's deep enough to dive?'

'I'm sure it is,' he answered recklessly, his mind divorced from his tongue.

She unwrapped her towel.

No teenager on his first priapic adventure could have known the tension he enjoyed as the moonlight picked out the details of her body before she raised her arms and dived. When she surfaced, she called out: 'What are you waiting for?'

He dropped his towel. He was a non-diver, so he jumped; he was a poor swimmer, but with a makeshift breaststroke, he could make some progress.

'This is like swimming in champagne,' she called out before, with expert strokes, she came up to where he laboured and for a brief moment their bodies touched. He reached out for her, forgetting the need to keep swimming, and sank. As he came to the surface, spluttering, arms and legs working hard, she laughed.

'I'm going to go around the nearest yacht,' she said.

He cursed his inability to follow her. This was the moment when a man needed to show he was the stronger . . .

As she disappeared behind the yacht, he found himself ridiculously hoping there was no one aboard who was watching her circling body. She rounded the stern and reappeared. When half-way across, she ceased swimming and floated. There was little movement in the water, yet her body rose and fell sufficiently for her secrets briefly to be revealed. After a while, she turned on her front and swam across to the landing stage; once more her body touched his and she was in no hurry to disengage. 'I think I've had enough for the moment. You'll have to help me out because it's too high to get up on my own.' She raised her arms and gripped the edge of the landing stage.

Her held her waist and pushed, promptly went under the water. She was laughing harder than before when he surfaced. Despite her earlier words, as he gained a fresh grip on her waist, she hauled herself up and her silken flesh slid through his hands.

She knelt, leaning over the edge, and her breasts became neat cones. 'D'you want a hand?'

Nothing would have persuaded him to admit such a need. Using all his strength, he hauled himself up out of the water and on to the landing stage, tried to conceal how breathless that had made him.

He stood, put his arms around her and drew her to him; as their bodies met, he slid his right hand down . . .

She wriggled free. She grasped his right hand and held it against her crutch. 'That's what you hoped you were going to enjoy, isn't it?' She moved herself against his hand. 'And were stupid enough to think it's this that I wanted.' She jerked his hand away.

'What . . .'

'What?' she repeated contemptuously.

'I thought . . .'

'Thought I'd like having your pig hands all over my body?'

'If you didn't want . . . why did you . . . ?' Bewildered, he struggled to find the words which might bring sense to the scene. 'You encouraged me to ask you out; when we drove over here from the restaurant, you didn't stop at the hotel to get a costume; in the water, you touched me and must have known how exciting that was. Why? Why if you didn't want me to . . . to . . .'

She laughed maliciously. 'You're a detective and still can't understand?'

'Of course I can't.'

'Then I'll have to explain. I've been enjoying myself because nothing is such fun, so satisfying as making a fool out of a man who thinks a woman is going to lie down in front of him with her legs apart; as getting him all excited and then disappointing him.' She picked up her towel and wrapped it around herself, crossed to the wooden steps and climbed them.

His humiliation was so great that had he had a gun, he would have been tempted to shoot either her or himself.

Twenty-Five

The family were asleep – at least, he hoped they were, because he needed to be on his own as he tried to fight through the bitterness. He emptied the glass, poured out another brandy, added several cubes of ice. He had already drunk sufficient to have given him the comfort of drunkenness normally, but he remained sober – alcohol was ever a false comforter.

It was easy to use hindsight to realize what a fool he had been from the very beginning. The clerk at the hotel had suggested Tabitha and Mary might be lesbians, but he had scorned the possibility because Tabitha had been with Muir. He should have wondered why Mary was so bad tempered when he was present and no doubt made it obvious how attracted he was to Tabitha; have tried to judge what kind of woman would deliberately cause her friend such jealous pain; should have asked himself why Tabitha would encourage a nearly middle-aged detective . . . and not avoided the question by assuring himself she had the character to appreciate values other than youth. He should have accepted that her behaviour was sufficiently unusual to raise questions . . . But of course he had done none of those things because he had seen himself in the clothes of Don Juan.

He drained the glass, refilled it. Now he knew why there had been a row between her and Muir, why Muir had returned downstairs that Saturday looking like a thunder-storm yet she had been smiling, why he had not driven her down to the port, but had ordered Ortiz to do that. She would have played a different hand (an infelicitous expression?) when dealing with a man of Muir's character than she had with him. There would have been no need to encourage, only to delay. She would have used innocence as a goad, have allowed hopeful familiarity and then, when the game began to bore, have humiliated. Muir's anger must have increased her enjoyment . . .

He put the glass down on the table. Muir, self-made, wealthy, unscrupulous, with a contempt for failure – how would such a man meet his own humiliating failure? Perhaps by trying to humiliate someone else, by assuaging his aroused passions on that someone?

He picked up the glass and emptied it. What had Dolores said the other day which he now sought to remember because he instinctively 'knew' her words suddenly held an importance he had not begun to recognize at the time? . . . Something about women being born to bear pain in silence while men had only to lose one drop of blood to call for help . . . Why hadn't Muir called for help after he'd been stabbed? The wound would have been painful and he must have known he suffered from a blood disorder that was potentially fatal. What in such circumstances would stop a man immediately taking steps to get medical help? The certainty he would have to explain how he had suffered the wounds? And had the answer to that question been so embarrassing, he had put off being faced by it until weakness overcame him and he could no longer appreciate it would be better to be embarrassed than to die? . . . If the significance of the absence of any cry for help had been understood – as, of course, it would have been by even a moderately clever detective – then the time at which the wound could have been inflicted would not, because Muir had specifically said nothing was wrong, have been accepted as necessarily after Ortiz and Elena had driven away from Sa Rotaga . . .

He poured another drink. It was small consolation to know he had solved the case because Tabitha had humiliated him.

'You will be very late at the office,' Dolores said, as Alvarez entered the kitchen.

He crossed to the table and sat.

'I called you three times.'

'I didn't hear you.'

'Hardly surprising. Do you want chocolate?'

'Just coffee. Black.'

'I have been out to buy some coca from the bakery run by Irene's cousin because she promised me it was always good and I have not had time to make any.'

'Not for me.'

'I bought it especially for you and now you tell me you don't want it?'

'I don't feel very well.'

She unscrewed the coffee maker and began to fill the bottom of this with water. 'I suppose you have a headache?'

'A real thumper.'

'And are feeling sick.' She spooned ground coffee into the container in the bottom half, screwed both halves together, put them on the stove and lit the gas.

'I won't go to the office. You can phone and tell them.'

'That you drank so much last night, you still count eight fingers and two thumbs on each hand?'

'I hardly drank anything.'

'Then the coñac evaporated from the bottle which was

full when I put it in the sideboard yesterday, yet was almost empty this morning when I found it on the table?'

'I may have had a couple of small drinks.'

'It is unusual to find a man making little of much instead of much of little . . . Do you think your friend will be fit enough to leave the island today?'

'What friend?'

'You have forgotten you told me yesterday evening you did not want the meal I had specially prepared for you because you were meeting someone with whom you had been at training school? . . . I did not, of course, believe that. I can always tell when you are lying.'

'How?'

'That is not something you need know. It was perfectly obvious you were rushing off to see your naked woman.'

'She was not—' She had been naked.

Dolores sniffed loudly. The coffee machine hissed and she turned off the gas, poured coffee into a mug. 'Are you capable of helping yourself to sugar and milk?'

'Of course I am,' he muttered.

'Then I will start cleaning the house, something I am very capable of doing since, being a woman, I practise restraint.'

He was feeling slightly better when he parked in front of Sa Rotaga. He opened the front door, entered, called out. Elena came through one of the far doorways. 'What do you want this time?' she asked in a tone which suggested that whatever it was, he would be denied.

'To ask you something.'

'Do you get paid by the number of questions you ask? . . . I suppose you'll want some coffee and coca.'

'Coffee, but no coca.'

'Because you've been drinking too heavily, from the look of you.'

Women had one-track minds.

They went through to the kitchen and he sat at the table. As she prepared the coffee machine, she said: 'When are me and Pablo going to learn what happens here?'

'If you mean, about your employment, I can't answer.'

'Because your brain is too scrambled?'

'Because it's up to the lawyers, not us.'

'Then we will have to wait for a blue moon before we know; with an estate this rich, the lawyers will gorge themselves before they bother with the likes of us.' Having measured out the coffee, she screwed down the top of the plastic container.

'I've come here to ask you to tell me what happened that Saturday.'

'I have told you.' She opened a cupboard and brought out two mugs.

'Not the truth.'

'You wish to call me a liar?' she demanded as she put the mugs down on the table.

'After the meal, which Tabitha didn't like, she and the señor went up to his bedroom. When they returned downstairs, she was cheerful, even laughing, but he was so furious he wouldn't drive her to the hotel. Why do you think that was?'

'I have no idea.'

'You can't guess? Pablo did.'

'Guesses come easily to a mind like his.'

'After she and Pablo left, what did the señor do?'

'How would I know?'

'Because it is a memory that will never leave you.'

'I've work to do. When the coffee makes, pour yourself what you want.'

236

'Why put two mugs on the table if you're not intending to drink? . . . Elena, you're going to have to tell me.'

'There's nothing to tell,' she said fiercely.

'The truth is, isn't it, that the señor watched them drive away and was so furious, so humiliated, and frustration so warped his mind that he tried to fondle you?'

She sat so suddenly, it was as if her legs had betrayed her.

'Tell me now, when we are on our own. If others hear you, I'll be unable to do anything to help.'

She was silent for a while, then said, speaking in a low voice. 'Lorenzo will never believe.'

'If you explain . . .'

'He won't understand.'

The older Mallorquins held inflexible views on marriage and faithfulness. A woman was either chaste or a puta. If a man sexually assaulted her, it must be her fault because she had encouraged him with lewd behaviour. Elena had often said how jealous her husband was. If she admitted Muir had tried to assault her sexually, Lorenzo would believe this was because she had encouraged Muir and probably nothing she could say would persuade him otherwise. He would reject her because she had disgraced him. 'Tell me exactly what happened and then we will work something out.'

She spoke unwillingly, constantly looking quickly at him to try to gauge whether he believed her or was contemptuously blaming her . . .

It had been obvious Muir was eager – so eager it had been embarrassing to see him with the puta. After the meal, the two of them had gone upstairs. Normally, he would have been calm when he returned downstairs, but that day he wasn't. The puta had been all smiles, he had been in the foulest of moods. Some time after Pablo had driven the puta to the hotel, she had been very carefully washing up the carving knife and fork which according to the señor were old and valuable, when he had come into the kitchen. She couldn't understand most of what he had said and because of his behaviour had judged him to be too drunk to know what he was doing . . . That was until, to her horror, he'd . . .

'Tell me.'

'I cannot.'

'You must.'

He'd reached for her breasts. Because he was the señor, she'd tried to shame him into stopping. But he'd . . .

'What did he do?'

He had run his hands under her skirt. She had struggled, but he was strong. Terrified, knowing only that she had to escape his raping her, her right hand had touched the carving fork. Not really conscious of what she was doing, she had stabbed him with it . . .

The unidentified weapon, unidentified because so few Mallorquins cooked a joint which needed carving – and if it did, they used a kitchen knife and an ordinary fork – that the forensic scientists had not thought, any more than he had, to consider a traditional foreign carving fork with curved prongs . . . Ironically, had Muir accepted Elena's choice for that meal, he would probably still be alive because there would have been no need to carve . . .

As Muir cried out, he released her, rushed out of the kitchen. Terrified, she had washed off the faint smudges of blood on the two prongs, dried the fork, put it and the carving knife in the velvet-lined case and the case in the drawer where it was kept. She had told Pablo to drive her home, even if it was early. They'd been in the car about to leave when the señor had appeared out of the house. She had been terrified he would say something which would make Pablo realize what had happened, but when Pablo had called out to know if the señor wanted something, all he'd done was shake his head . . .

At first, she could not believe she had been responsible for the señor's death. The carving fork had not gone in very deeply and had he not appeared in the courtyard and denied anything was wrong? . . . Later, she had learned about the blood disorder and she had had to understand perhaps she had been responsible and from that moment she had been tormented by fear that her guilt would become known and Lorenzo would throw her out of the house because he would never believe she had done nothing to encourage the señor . . .

'We must prevent your husband ever knowing what happened,' Alvarez said.

'How?' she asked wildly.

'I'll think of something,' he answered recklessly.

Twenty-Six

On Monday morning, Alvarez sat in his office and bitterly accepted that since Elena had been responsible for Muir's death, the law would condemn her. He had promised to find a way in which her husband would never learn what had happened, but now had to accept his words were as valueless as last week's copy of *El Dia*. If Locke's innocence was to be established, as it must be, Elena's part in Muir's death must become known. Lives were going to be ruined because a man who had deserved to die, had died at the hands of innocence.

The phone interrupted his black thoughts.

'Elisabeth Vaillant, Police Judicaire, Perpignan,' said a woman in passable Spanish. 'I have a report on Alain Escoffier . . .'

'On who?' he asked, his mind temporarily blank.

She repeated the name.

'I'm afraid I don't quite understand . . .'

'You are not Inspector Alvarez of the Cuerpo General de Policia?'

'Yes.'

'Then did you not ask this department to make enquiries to find out if someone by the name of Escoffier, who was wealthy, had a fairly close Spanish relative, and had recently died, came from this area?'

Memory flooded back and he hurriedly tried to cover

240

his stupidity. 'The trouble is, we have in hand enquiries concerning a man who, by an extraordinary coincidence, has the same name, Escoffier, and since he is not known ever to have left the island or to have had any contact with France, I could not understand why you would be giving me a report on him. My apologies.'

'Quite understandable. . . We identified an Alain Escoffier, but whether he is the person you're interested in, you will have to judge because far from being rich, he was not very well off and his estate, which is not expected to amount to more than a hundred and twenty thousand euros, has been willed to a part-time housekeeper who has been with him for several years. He did, however, often boast of a Spanish cousin who lived on one of the Balearic islands and held high office in the local government.'

With a flash of cosmic brilliance, his dark world had become suffused with golden light. He would not have denied that a Hollywood choir began to sing. He thanked her for the information, praised the work of the Judiciaire, said that the co-operation between the two countries was an example to the world, and indeed became so fulsome that she brought the conversation to an abrupt end, fearing his loquacity portended a move into non-official matters . . .

After replacing the receiver, he pulled open the bottom right-hand drawer of the desk and brought out the bottle of brandy and a glass, poured out the first drink to salute the French detectives who had worked so successfully, the second to salute himself for his bloody-minded determination to ignore orders.

He rang Palma.

'Yes?' said the secretary with the plummy voice.

'I should like to speak to the superior chief.'

'He is very busy.'

'It is a matter of considerable importance.'

'Wait.'

He stared at his empty glass.

'What do you want?' demanded Salas.

'Señor, something has occurred which I fear may have very serious consequences for the reputation of the Cuerpo. It concerns an officer and how he will be judged if it becomes known he was given adverse information concerning a prominent person which he chose to disbelieve, despite the proof that it was true, on grounds which have turned out to be false. Is it not likely that in such circumstances there will be those who will believe he would not accept the truth in order to ingratiate himself with that person of power?'

'What the devil have you been up to now?'

'This does not refer to me, Señor.'

'Then who?'

'You.'

There was a pause before Salas shouted: 'You've taken leave of your senses! This is too much to bear for any man, however broad-minded. Consider yourself suspended from duty as from this moment.'

'Señor, I think you should know that I have just been informed on unimpeachable authority that Señor Yague's cousin has recently died, but he was far from a rich man, no large amount of cash was found in his house, and in any case his estate is willed to a part-time housekeeper. The story Señor Yague gave you was a lie from beginning to end. You will remember that there was evidence to suggest this was so, but you decided to ignore that and believe the minister. Naturally, anyone who knows you would never suggest this was because you thought that by doing so, you would promote your career, but sadly it has to be accepted that small-minded persons, of whom there are so many, may well believe that, should the facts ever become known.'

'But he . . . When a minister . . .' Salas came to a halt.

'Señor, you may well be reluctant to listen to any suggestion I might make, but while it is naturally recognized truth must normally face the glare of publicity, a reasonable person will surely accept there may be a time when for the sake of the innocent, it should remain in the shadows. I have been trying to solve the riddle of Señor Muir's death, yet even after days, weeks of extremely hard work, I am forced to confess I can find nothing further to inculpate Señor Locke. Since no further evidence against him has come to light, one has to face the fact that perhaps this is because there is none – he is innocent, however much the known facts appear to accuse him. Then, one has to ask, who else might the guilty person be? All those who can be considered suspect can be shown to be innocent. This would appear to leave the case wide open until one accepts that occasionally a negative becomes a positive. If no one can be suspected of stabbing Señor Muir, then it has to be the case he accidentally fell on to something which inflicted the wounds. What that something was is still a mystery. But life and death are full of mysteries.

'As you perhaps remember, during the course of my investigation, it appeared there had been a case of bribery and Señor Muir was involved in an attempt to persuade the minister to grant development permission of the Wilderness. Should a finding of accidental death not be acceptable and investigations into Señor Muir's death have to continue, I cannot see how one can avoid all the details concerning the money in the safe coming to light. It would then become generally known that at the minister's insistence, you gave orders no further enquiries were to be made regarding this, despite the weight of evidence. I know you acted as a man of honour in accepting the word of someone you unfortunately mistook to be another man of honour, but I wonder whether others will be so able to judge where the truth lies? Will they not wonder why you rejected the evidence? As I have already mentioned—'

'Then don't mention it again . . . You said . . . Alvarez, earlier, you seemed to suggest there might be some way out of this ghastly situation?'

'I think the one person who might unwittingly cause a full investigation to become inevitable is Diego Vives because of his desire to sell his aunt's land. If I spoke to him and explained that should the land be sold when his aunt, who is known to be a conservationist, is incapable of understanding what is going on, he will be charged with theft, fraud, and perhaps a few other offences, I am sure that, being of a cowardly nature, he will decide not to pursue a sale to another party. Beyond that, one must always allow for the unexpected. Therefore, the minister should make certain no suspicion of blame can ever touch him and surely this can best be achieved by his giving to charity a sum of money noticeably larger than three hundred thousand euros – the exact amount could lead to uncharitable conclusions – and making it clear he had never begun to consider allowing development of the Wilderness; further, in order to underline his determination there never shall be any, he should promote a law to the effect that the land is forever to remain undeveloped.'

Eventually, Salas said: 'I have been underestimating your capabilities. Unfortunately, those in which you excel are not ones the Cuerpo welcomes.' He slammed down the receiver.

Alvarez relaxed as he considered what remained to be done. Elena must learn Lorenzo would never know what

244

had happened that Saturday; Locke must be told he was no longer a suspect. Was there any pleasure greater than bringing an end to fear? Especially when Locke served rather a good coñac . . .

Appendix: Mallorquin Recipes,
Courtesy of Dolores

TONYINA AMB SAFRA (TUNA WITH SAFFRON RICE)

4 large fresh tuna steaks
2 onions
3-4 cloves of garlic
1 egg yolk
1-2 glasses of white wine
Scrap of lemon peel
¼ cup of olive oil
½ cup of pine nuts
Parsley, bay leaf, pepper, salt & pinch of saffron

Method
Fry tuna in very hot olive oil till coloured on both sides.
Add onions over a low heat, and garlic cloves, cook until
onions are soft. Turn off heat. Stir in egg yolk (previously
beaten), white wine and pine nuts, slice of lemon peel, one
bay leaf, saffron and season to taste. Cook over a very low
heat for 10-15 minutes.

LLENGUA AMB TÁPERES (TONGUE WITH CAPERS)

1 calf's tongue (1lb / 1.5 kg)
4 peeled & diced onions
3 tomatoes skinned, diced and seeded

4 leaves of sorrel
2 sticks of celery plus green leaves
3 oz capers
Salt, pepper, cinnamon, bay leaf, chopped parsley
Pork lard

Method
Wash tongue. Cook in well-lidded saucepan from cold with salt. Cook over medium heat for about 45 minutes. When cooked rinse with cold water and remove skin. Keep stock. Briefly fry the tongue on all sides in the lard. Add onions, tomatoes, sorrel, celery, bay leaf, pepper and one tablespoon of chopped parsley. Simmer all together for half an hour. Remove the tongue. Sieve all the other ingredients or cream with liquidizer. Add capers and a little cinnamon to taste. Slice the tongue and pour the sauce over it.

OBLADES AMB BOLETS (TURBOT AND MUSHROOMS)

1 large fillet of turbot per person (suggest for 4 persons)
12 oz peeled and sliced mushrooms
1 chopped onion
½ cup of olive oil
1 cup of white wine
1 lemon
Salt
Parsley

Method
Cover a large frying pan with coarse salt about ¼″ deep, heat until the salt is hot. Put fish on to salt to grill for about 6 minutes. Skin the fish and put on a hot plate. Fry chopped

onions in olive oil, add mushrooms and parsley. Put into casserole, place turbot fillets on mushrooms, add wine and lemon juice. Heat all together for about 15 minutes.

ESCALDUMS DE GALLINA (CHICKEN COOKED IN ALMOND SAUCE)

1 chicken, cut into 8 parts
½ cup of ground toasted almonds
1 hard-boiled egg
1 cup of olive oil
3-4 cloves (according to taste) of crushed garlic
1 dessert spoon of finely chopped parsley
Pinch of saffron
Salt and pepper
Chicken stock

Method
Sauté chicken in olive oil until light brown. Add a little chicken stock, parsley and garlic. Simmer on a low gas. Mix ground almonds with yolk of hard-boiled egg. Mix with chicken, garlic, parsley, chicken stock and saffron. Salt and pepper to taste. Put into a casserole with a tight lid and cook slowly in oven, Gas No. 4 or 175 degrees (C), moderate temperature, until cooked. After about an hour, add more chicken stock, to give a good sauce. Serve with boiled potatoes and green vegetables.

XULLA DEL CEL (RICH CUSTARD)

2 cups of castor sugar

20 (shades of Mrs Beeton) egg yolks
Water

Method
Dissolve sugar in 1 cup of water. Cook for about 3
minutes, with lid off saucepan. Remove from heat when
syrup forms threads from spoon. Cool slightly. Add single
egg yolks until a smooth mix is obtained. Pour into a mould,
previously greased with a little butter. Put mould in a bowl
of water and then both into a slow oven for about half an
hour until set. Leave to cool before turning out. Can also be
cooked in a dish and served direct without turning out.